D0132345

ANYONE BUT HER

LISA LACE

JACK

IT'S NOT when I take my first breath of fresh Maryland air that I feel free; not when I look back over my shoulder to see the walls of North Branch Correctional Institution standing behind me for the last time. It's not until the moment both my feet are firmly planted on the other side of the front gate that I feel the weight of incarceration lifted from my shoulders.

A hundred yards outside the prison a car is waiting for me. It's a beat-up, rusty old 1975 Ford Pinto, and leaning casually back against the hood is my old cellmate, Sparky. He hasn't aged much in the four years since I last saw him. His dark hair is still slicked back and scraggly. He's wearing scuffed denim jeans and a plain, oversized black T-shirt; both filthy as if he's just come from working at a body shop when I know for a fact he's probably done nothing else today but watch crappy daytime TV and smoke joints.

"Strike!" He calls my name as he pushes himself off the hood of the car and staggers my way with his iconic swagger. He lights a cigarette as he approaches, taking a deep drag just before he pulls me into an uncomfortable hug with one arm. "Not looking bad, mate. I'd say you still don't look a day over twenty-one."

"Not so sure about that. Fourteen years in that place has done its damage."

"The rough edges suit you." He jerks his head towards the Pinto. "We getting out of here or what? The sight of this place is making my skin crawl."

"For sure." The Pinto's door groans when I pull it open. It feels almost like the whole thing will fall off in my hand. "Is this the same car you had before you got arrested?"

Sparky laughs, the sound husky in his throat from years of chain smoking. "This old gal has never done me wrong."

"Looks like she spent all ten of those years sitting in the rain."

"And she still purrs like a kitten."

The sound that emerges from the battered engine is not exactly what I'd describe as a purr. It's more like cogs grinding in a broken machine.

Sparky drives. The landscape rolls past. I thought everything outside the prison would look like an explosion of color after fourteen years inside, but the world still seems to be painted in shades of gray. I slump down in my seat, a crease forming in my forehead as I frown.

"What's wrong with you?" Sparky asks. "You should be, like, crazy happy right now. I remember when I got out, the first thing I did was go straight to the Twilight Bar and blow two hundred dollars on booze and gals. I hadn't seen a woman's ass in ten years. What say we head there right now? I'll even buy your first dance."

"It's two p.m. on a Tuesday."

"That just means there'll be more girls to go around."

"I'm good, thanks. Got to protect what little cash I've got left."

"You didn't have anything squirreled away? I thought you said you had a nest egg?"

"If you call two grand a nest egg." I squeeze my eyes shut and rub my temples. "You think you've served your time, but the punishment goes on."

"You could probably put down a deposit on some little studio in Baltimore with that."

"Yeah? And then what? What's the point in signing up to a lease with a rent I could never afford? I haven't got a job, and nobody's going to hire an ex-con who's served fourteen years for manslaughter. Hell, I probably wouldn't get a landlord to take me on, either. I don't even have a car to sleep in."

"Good thing you've got your old pal Sparky to sort you out then, isn't it?"

I smile. "Thanks, Sparky. They've been on my back about an address for that release form for weeks. I had to say I had somewhere to go."

He takes another drag from his cigarette and throws the butt out the window. "I'll even put up with the spot-checks from parole—for you. Got a secret place sorted for my junk so we'll both look like good little boys when the Man comes knocking."

I think back to when I first met Sparky on day one in the joint. He'd been just a few years older than me, sentenced to ten years for a series of fires he'd set off all throughout Baltimore. His run of arson caught up with him when an elderly woman sleeping in an apartment block didn't make it out in time. If he ever felt any guilt for killing her, he never let it show.

If you'd have asked me before all this began whether I'd have ever come to rely on a pyromaniac junkie as my one and only friend in the world, I'd have told you my future was brighter than that. I was very wrong.

"Don't mention it. What else am I going to do? Let you

sleep on the streets? Isn't like you've got anyone else to go home to. No chick waiting for you, no brothers or sisters. Hell, you haven't even got a momma to go back to."

"Thanks for summarizing that for me, Sparky. Makes me feel just"—I take in a deep breath, then let it all out on the next word—"great."

"I'm not judging, man. I'm in the same boat."

"I thought you had three brothers?"

"All behind bars, my friend. You're the closest thing I've got to a brother on the outside." He grins. "I'm psyched you're finally out." He slams his palm on the steering wheel in excitement. "You sure you don't want to hit up the Twilight Bar?"

"I just want a hot shower and a cold beer."

"Well, my shower ain't great, and my fridge has blown a fuse—still, a lukewarm shower and a warm beer are better than showering with a load of other dudes and eating that prison junk."

"I can't remember the last time I had a real drink."

"I've got more than beer to offer you. A couple of lines and you'll be feeling on top of the world."

"You know I'm not into all that stuff."

"Are you kidding? It's a celebration!"

"I don't know. Somehow, I've got to try and salvage some kind of life after all this."

"You know, I can hook you up with some work. A job."

I perk up. "Oh yeah? What kind of work?"

Sparky's smile is mischievous. "This and that."

"Not honest work, then?"

He laughs. "There's no such thing."

"I'm going down the straight and narrow. Ending up in prison in the first place was a huge mistake that I've paid for with fourteen years of my life. I'm still young—I'm only thirty-five. I can still make something of myself."

"What? With that crappy art course you did inside?"

"I was getting pretty good at it."

Sparky scoffs. "You killed a man, Strike. That doesn't go away just because you've done your time. You're a convict for life; you've just stepped onto the merry-go-round—jumping through hoops to keep parole, having to account for every minute of your time, getting turned away from every decent job because that black mark's against your name. It's well and good thinking you're going to be the one that takes the high road, but with nobody out there to give you a step up, you're going to have to take the help you can get; even if it comes from people in low places."

I slump down further in my seat and turn my miserable gaze out the window. I never intended to be a criminal. I had dreams to get out of Baltimore and be someone, but life threw too many curve balls my way, and I struck out.

The car smells like stale smoke and body odor. We've got as far as Berkeley Springs; there's a market on in the street. People are buying flowers and artisan candles, indulging in handmade luxuries while I wonder how the hell I'm meant to salvage some kind of life out of this shit-heap of an existence.

Sparky looks across at me, his expression softening slightly. "Look, Jack—" He uses my real name. "You can take more than one route to the same place, you know? Just because you get your hands dirty at first, doesn't mean you can't get that fairytale clean-as-a-whistle life you're dreaming of down the line. But you've got to start somewhere. Cash can cover a multitude of sins."

I lift my hand. "Enough. I can't talk about this right now. Let me have one day to just enjoy being free."

"You're right. Sit back and relax, my friend. I'm going to get you back to my place, crack open a couple of beers, and if you're lucky, I might even throw a couple of dogs on the barbeque. It's going to be a warm night."

"That sounds good. It's been forever since I just sat outside."

"Put the memories of cell life behind you. Your new life starts today, my friend."

MEGAN

THERE IS A DULL, aching pain in my feet that makes it feel like I'm walking on cobbles. I'm practically limping by the time I make it to my front door after a ten-hour shift cutting hair in Fell's Point, Baltimore. There's pain between my thumb and fingers from where I've been snipping with scissors all day. All I want to do is put my feet up and have a glass or two of cheap wine.

As I round the corner onto Marlen Street, I know that's not going to happen. Two men sharply dressed in business suits are standing at the bottom of the three steps that lead up to my apartment block. I'm suspicious for two reasons—firstly, nobody around here goes to work in a suit; secondly, they're acting like they're on lookout.

The first man—a forty-something-year-old man of Middle Eastern descent—keeps scanning up and down the street like he's expecting trouble. He keeps one hand on the radio receiver on his belt, ready to call in any signs of trouble.

His companion—a younger man in his mid-thirties—looks more casual, but when he places his hands in his pockets, his suit jacket pulls back and I can see a gun holster on his hip. Gangsters and policemen don't dress like that. These are US marshals—and I bet I know why they're here.

I tighten my grip on my purse, take a deep breath, and walk on bravely toward them. They both perk up when they spot me and turn in my direction.

"Miss Cartwright?"

"Yes."

The first marshal holds out his hand to shake mine. "I'm Senior Inspector Khosa. This is Senior Inspector Kroft. We're from WITSEC—The Witness Security program. May we come inside?"

"I didn't think we'd discuss this in the street. Yes, come in." I fumble with my keys in the lock. My hands feel numb; my blood is like lead in my veins. After I'd escaped Calvin and not heard from him in the last six weeks, I thought I'd escaped. I should have known better. *What has he got me into now?*

Inspector Khosa takes the key from me. "Let me." His voice is soft and comforting; he has kind eyes and a reassuring presence.

"You must be used to people freaking out when you show up."

"We are indeed, ma'am. Not to worry. We're going to guide you through this process every step of the way."

I stop speaking as I step into the foyer of the apartment block and see Kerry with her two kids and bags full of groceries. I see her eyes dart to the two men behind me, and she quickly ushers her boys inside. *Everybody knows I was Calvin's girl.*

A lump rises in my throat. I was a victim as Calvin's girlfriend, and I've been a pariah ever since I walked away. I stride up the stairs toward the third story.

"Sorry for the walk, gentlemen. The elevator's been out of order since I moved in." I turn back over my shoulder to look at the marshals. "I'm guessing I won't have to put up with it much longer?"

"We'll talk when we're inside."

I shake my head; there's a bitter taste in my mouth. "That bastard stole my youth, and now he's going to rip away the semblance of a life I've managed to claw out for myself."

I open my apartment door, and the three of us step inside. I see both men taking in my little haven, and I lift my chin defiantly against any shame that might creep in. Everything I have is shabby and second-hand, but I bought every item with my own money off the back of my own hard work. This place and the things in it are *mine* and mine alone.

"Well, here we are. Tell me what's going on." I fold my arms over my chest and stare at the two marshals, right there in the tiny slither of hall between my apartment door and living room, my shoes piled up against the wall, the three of us cramped in. I don't offer them coffee or take them to sit down. It took everything in me to make it up the stairs without demanding an explanation. I can't wait any longer.

"Somebody has broken confidence."

"What does that mean?"

Senior Inspector Khosa puts a hand on my shoulder. "Someone has spoken. We have reason to believe Calvin Raynor knows you plan to testify against him."

My head spins. I stumble back a step but quickly regain my balance. "Come in." I go to my sofa in my living room, not even caring about the sweater crumpled on the floor or the half-empty glass of wine still on the coffee table from last night. I sink down into the cushions.

Inspector Kroft sits beside me and bows his head to catch my eye. "It's understandable that you're afraid."

"Afraid?" I scowl. "I'm furious. I really thought this time I'd got away, but Calvin never lets anyone turn their back on him. He's the king of the streets and an emperor in his own mind." I lift my hands. "So, what happens now?"

"We recommend witness protection."

I nod slowly. "What does that involve?"

"You pack up tonight—right now—and you come with us," Inspector Khosa tells me. "We'll take you to the airport. I'll join you on the plane and take you right to the door of your new life. A fresh start, a new identity."

"A new birth certificate, new passport, new social security number," Inspector Kroft adds. "A new name. A new person. Megan Cartwright disappears forever. Somebody new starts a life in a new state, safe to live a happy life."

Inspector Khosa leans forward. "I understand this is a hard decision, but Calvin Raynor is one of the most dangerous men in America. His reach is larger than we could imagine. Your best chance of survival is getting far away from here and leaving everything you knew behind."

"Survival?" I pick up the half-drunk leftover wine and take a sip. I look down at the carpet, staring at navy spots of fluff on the beige fibers from where my fluffy socks were planted last night. "You think Calvin would kill me?"

"He's wanted for three murders—that we know of," Inspector Kroft says. "We know this is a man capable of killing, and this wouldn't be the first time a potential witness disappeared when the feds were circling in around Raynor."

"You've been in his inner circle for years. You know Calvin better than anyone, and you're the best chance the prosecution has of putting him away for a very long time. He's smart enough to know that."

"You're in danger, Megan."

Kroft, Khosa, Kroft....my eyes dart from one to the other as they give their rehearsed speech.

I run my finger pensively around the rim of my wine glass. "Danger is nothing new to me. You're right—I was in Calvin's inner circle, and I've seen things that would make your skin crawl; things you wouldn't believe."

"You were as much a victim of Raynor's tyranny as anyone else," Kroft says firmly. "You were scared for your life."

"Was I?" I put the glass back down and bite my lip. "It's all so hazy now. Did I stay out of love or fear? I hardly know anymore."

Khosa frowns. "It was fear when you ran into that police station with blood on your shirt. It was fear when you refused to leave the station after you gave your statement because you were terrified he'd be waiting outside. Nobody doubts you're a tough cookie, Miss Cartwright, but you were about as scared as any victim I've ever met."

"I'm not a victim, Inspector Khosa. I'm a witness. There is a difference."

"You're saying Raynor never laid a hand on you?"

"I'm saying I could have come forward much sooner." Guilt gnaws at my stomach once again; it's a feeling as familiar as hunger or fatigue to me now. Every time I pause to think about the things I saw without speaking up, my insides crawl with self-hatred. *I should have done more.*

"You're not on trial, Miss Cartwright," Khosa says. "The law has determined you were an unwilling participant in Raynor's crimes. You didn't hurt anyone; you never killed anyone. There's no record of you stealing or committing fraud, or knowing anything about the kidnapping. Anything you might have done is far outweighed by the good you've done in coming forward. Your courage may very well take a very dangerous man off the streets for good."

"Don't be mistaken; there is blood on my hands." My eyelids flutter against the tears welling in my eyes. "If I had come forward sooner, Aiden would still be here."

The newest member of Calvin's gang had been young and naïve. He'd been pulled in by his older brother but had no idea what he'd walked into until it was too late. I saw Calvin circling in on him, ready to make an example, and I kept quiet. It was no surprise to me when he finally pulled that trigger and ended the life of a young man just wanting to find somewhere to belong. Hadn't I made the very same mistake in letting Calvin take me under his wing? Nineteen years old and desperate to find a corner of the world to call my own. I was like a moth to the flame.

The first three years flew by—it was one big, exciting, adrenaline-fueled, rebellious adventure. Then Calvin made a name for himself. Petty crime turned into assault, murder, and kidnapping. The adventure became a nightmare. The last eight years have dragged by; a slow, torturous walk through hell.

Inspector Khosa moves the conversation along. "We can't stay here long, Miss Cartwright. Here's what you need to understand.

"If you come with us, we will take you to a safe place, give you a new identity, and provide you protection before, during, and after Raynor's trial. You will be unidentifiable, safe, and under supervision from men who are trained to protect you.

"But for us to offer this lifeline, you have to make a difficult choice: leave everything and everyone you know behind. You will have to cut off all contact with everyone you know—family, friends, colleagues. There will be no phone calls, no Skype, no letters, no emails. Nobody can ever know where you've gone or who you've become."

I wet my dry lips. "For how long?"

"Nobody can force you to stay in the program," Inspector Kroft explains, "but the second you return to your old life, you risk being targeted and we won't be able to protect you."

"This is bigger than you, Megan," Khosa tells me. "If you aren't kept safe until the trial, then your testimony will get nowhere. Calvin will be free to carry on his violent, sadistic ways; murdering without any kind of repercussions. Someone has to take this monster down. Right now, you're the only one who can make that happen."

"So it's my testimony you're protecting?" I lean back in my chair. "That's a little depressing. Then again, what does the life of a gang lord's ex-girlfriend really mean? I've not done anything else with my life."

Khosa dodges my statement. "We need an answer, Miss Cartwright."

I slap my hands down on my knees and stand. "Of course I'm coming. I've not survived eleven years with that maniac to die when I'm this close to getting away. What can I take?"

"The bare minimum. We want to be discreet. We'll take you to a staff entrance at the airport and keep you out of sight on the plane."

"Where are we going?"

"I can't tell you that yet."

"Fine."

Kroft stands beside me and follows me to my room as I go to pack. "Just what do you think I'm going to do, Inspector?"

"I need to make sure you don't contact anyone."

"Like who?" I let out a bitter laugh. "I haven't spoken to my parents in years. They disowned me after I took off with Calvin. No siblings. No friends. Everybody I ever knew is loyal to Calvin, and I can't blame them for staying away from me now. The last thing anybody wants to do is pick the wrong side and end up just like Aiden."

I shove handfuls of clothes and shoes into a bag. I leave my passport, my bank cards, and everything else with my name on. *Everything will be new.*

"How will I support myself in this new life?" I ask. "Will I get a job? Can I do that?"

"Eventually," Kroft says. "But to start off with, you'll be given a stipend to live on."

"As easy as that?"

"Nothing about this will be easy, Miss Cartwright. You're going to be looking over your shoulder for a long time."

"I'm already looking over my shoulder anyway."

I finish throwing things into my carryall and then follow the marshals back to their low-key black car outside. I get into the back passenger seat with Khosa at my side and hardly give a passing backward glance to the apartment block as we drive away.

I'm not sorry to leave that old life behind. Calvin may have just given me the best gift I ever got—a fresh start.

JACK

WILLIAM ELLIS TRIES HARD, but my god is he a bore. The twenty-something freshly anointed parole officer speaks like a parrot who swallowed the handbook on rehabilitation. He speaks to me like he's a cross between a therapist and Jesus himself, offering me cut-and-paste advice from his college textbooks.

I'm glad to be done with him and almost back at Sparky's.

I push open the door to his run-down former crack-house condo in one of the back streets of Baltimore and call out to him. "I'm back. Jesus Christ was that a ballache!"

Sparky appears around the doorframe, a beer in one hand and a packet of chips in the other. "Parole?"

"Yeah."

"Did you get a big old check mark for being a good boy this week?"

I frown. "It's a waste of everybody's time."

He tilts his beer toward me with a knowing expression. "Didn't I tell you? You'll be jumping through hoops for the rest of your life."

"It wouldn't be so bad if I could just find work. I want to feel like I'm part of the world again."

I take a look around Sparky's sleazy, dirty condo. One of the panels in the living room window must have broken at some time or another; now there's just a sheet of plywood covering it. The sofa is covered in mysterious stains and smells of stale smoke. The carpet has never seen a vacuum in its life, and I don't dare set foot on it without a pair of thick-soled shoes as it's sticky like the floor of a nightclub from years of spilled drinks and god knows what else.

Instead of drapes at the windows, a black sheet is pinned up by one corner, a thumbtack stuck above the window frame to pin up the other side at night. The rotting blanket I sleep under is crumpled on the floor next to the sofa; it's thin and ragged and only smells marginally better after a double spin at the launderette.

I don't want this to be my life.

"I spent hours at the damned library scouring want ads." I can't keep the exasperation out of my voice.

Sparky hands me a beer. I chip off the cap on the broken edge of the coffee table where a thousand caps have been popped before.

I continue my rant. "Every job these days wants two years' experience—and it's not like I'm aiming high. I'm looking at warehouse work, bar work; all kinds of menial jobs where I thought an ex-con might stand half a chance."

Sparky perches on the arm of the sofa at my side and slaps my shoulder. "Are you surprised? The world never gave you nothing before you got convicted; why would it give you anything now? Guys like us have to live outside the system because the system won't ever make room for us."

"You're saying I should sell guns on street corners and start running drugs?"

"All I'm saying is that maybe you're not going to fit back

into society just like that." He snaps his fingers. "You want to find your feet again. I get that. But to get anywhere, you've got to have something to start with. A little cash to get the ball rolling."

"I don't want to go down that path, Sparky. I should never have gone down it in the first place."

Sparky scoffs. "You were never going to be a college boy, Strike. You were never going to work in an office in some fancy suit or marry some well-to-do gal. You were born into this shitheap of a town to parents who couldn't give a fuck, and we both know most poor bastards who are born here, die here. Did you really think you'd be one of the magic few to break out?"

"I might have stood half a chance if Donnie fucking Reid had never come into our lives."

"You mean the violent drunk your mother let beat the shit out of you for years?"

"Stop talking about her."

"Oh yeah. I forgot you did what you did for her." He rolls his tongue around his teeth and sighs exaggeratedly in contempt. "Who wouldn't stick up for a gem of a woman like that?"

I stand up and step away from Sparky. His smugness and the fact he's absolutely right is making my skin crawl. I threw my life away out of loyalty to a mother who'd never put me first; a woman who continued to betray me even after I was behind bars.

Sparky stands too and follows me to the other side of the room. The rusting radiator behind me is making a pained sound, like a chained animal. It's groaning like a beast in agony.

"Look," he says calmly, "I'm not judging you. We've all been bitten by loyalty at one time or another. In the end, a man's got to learn to look after himself. Put himself first.

Well, most of the time. That's not to say a guy won't help a friend in need from time to time."

"What are you getting at?"

"I know of a job with your name on it. One big job; a huge payout. Enough to start afresh and put all this behind you. You could get out of Baltimore, get old Forger George to whip you up some docs; start again."

"Whatever you're selling, I'm not buying."

"Not even for a 150K payout?"

"Any job paying that kind of money is not the sort of thing I want to get involved in."

Sparky fixes me with a withering stare. "There's already blood on your hands."

"And it cost me everything."

"One kill to lose it all, one kill to get it all back."

"A kill?"

He nods, circling around me like a vulture, his usually dull eyes growing bright. He's got a twitch in his eye like he's been snorting coke again. He can't stay still, and he's half the weight he was in the slammer. I can count his ribs exposed underneath his loose, dirty white T-shirt. He never tried to make a clean break from a life of crime.

"Long story short, there's this guy—head of a gang I have some dealings with—well, he's got a court date set, and he's been able to convince most witnesses it's in their best interests not to testify. He's paid off a couple of his cronies to take the fall to account for some of the evidence. He's in a position, almost, where he can walk away from every allegation."

"But there's one he can't buy off?"

"There's one he wouldn't risk trying. She knows too much."

"She?"

"An ex-girlfriend. She's walked in his inner circle for years. She knows the names and faces of all his associates. She's seen all sorts of *activity*. She took off and now this man feels...*uneasy*. He'd sleep better if she was no longer around."

"He's looking for a hitman for his ex?" I shake my head. "I'm not your man. I'm not getting involved in a murder."

"She's no angel, Strike. This girl is bad news. You'd have to be to cozy up with a psycho like this."

"And what's to say this psycho wouldn't kill the hitman after the job was done?"

"He wouldn't need to. Nobody admits to being paid off by him, admits to pulling the trigger. It's not in the self-interest of the person to turn him in."

"A hundred-and-fifty grand for this kill." There's a bitter taste in my mouth. Is that all a human life is worth these days? "If it's such a good job, why aren't you taking it?"

"Three degrees of separation, my friend."

"Am I supposed to know what that means?"

Sparky settles back down onto the sofa. The sight of his bare feet on the putrid carpet turns my stomach. The dirt on his soles has migrated almost up to his ankles.

"When a crime is committed, who're the first people to get questioned? The main suspect, and then everyone he knows. So you don't get someone you know to do the job. You get someone you've never met to do it. Someone you don't know. Someone who doesn't know you."

"I'm not interested—and I don't think you should be involved either. Neither of us are killers."

"Both of us are killers, Jack."

"There's a difference between self-defense and murder."

"What you did wasn't self-defense. You wanted him dead."

I don't answer. I simply drink deeply from my bottle. "I'm not going to murder some girl I've never met."

"I've heard she's a real piece of work. She was this guy's right-hand man before she left him. Used to handle a gun like Bonnie Parker."

"Drop it. I'm not interested."

Sparky shrugs and walks away, leaving me feeling agitated. I'm not a killer. The man who died at my hands died for good reason, and if I had the chance, I'd kill him again—but that doesn't mean I'm out for blood. All that violence is behind me now.

Still, as the days pass, my desperation grows. Each day with Sparky brings its own troubles. There are constantly meth heads and down-and-outs traipsing in and out with their drugs and illegal guns. I have no choice but to turn a blind eye, but as each day passes, I get more and more disillusioned with it all. *What's the point in taking the high road if this is where it leads?*

I think about Sparky's offer a lot. I think about whether I could really take a stranger's life; I think about whether this woman deserves to die. If she's a soulless gangster's gunwoman, then maybe I'd be doing the world a favor by taking her out and righting the wrong that was done to me the day my mother brought Donnie into our lives.

As rejection letter after rejection letter piles in, and as I spend night after night surrounded by strangers off their heads, the bitterness and resentment grow to a point where I snap.

Four weeks out of prison and the darkness has called me right back in.

"Sparky—tell me more about this job."

MEGAN

I WRITE my new name out once more. *Tammy Miller*. I've been writing it daily for a month now, hoping that if I write it down enough times, it will start to feel like my own name. I've perfected my signature; I've cut my hair. I've got the birth certificate, passport, and social security number of this fake person. I'm living the life of a fictional woman. And I feel like a fiction myself.

My new home—Tammy's new home—is a little 2-bed condo in Galena, Illinois. Galena is a cute town, a place of history and culture. I pass much of my time walking around the Galena Historic District, looking at the historic landmarks like the Ulysses S. Grant Home and the Old Market House. It makes me feel like I've gone back in time; and in a way, I have—Tammy Miller is innocent. It's like I can be the girl I was when I was fifteen before rebellion kicked in and before I started to go down the wrong path. Only a few short years later, I'd meet Calvin and start down the road to hell.

I sigh and slam shut the notepad. I curl up on the window seat which overlooks the street outside and spend a few moments watching the citizens of Galena going about their business.

The condo is gorgeous; much nicer than anything I've ever lived in before. It's decorated neutrally, but I've already added a few feminine touches, like floral cushions on the window seat and heart-print crockery in the kitchen cupboards. It even smells nice; like fresh paint and lavender.

Most of my days are lazy ones now. Apart from handing out my fake resumé, there's not much for me to do but wait for the time to pass. As I promised, I've had no contact with anyone from my old life. I make use of the stipend the witness protection program provides to visit museums, buy baking ingredients, and drink coffee.

In fact, the bright light of the sunshine outside draws me from my perch. Just one block over is the sweetest little café where I often go now to sit and let the time go by in the company of others. Of course, I don't talk to anyone; I don't reach out. But it makes me feel a little more real to be somewhere where other people go.

On my way, I buy a national paper, then go to the café and take my usual spot at the table bar that overlooks the street outside. I order a latte. When it arrives, I sip it slowly while scouring the paper for any news on Calvin and the trial.

Last week I read that Pete had been found dead. Pete was far from a friend, but I knew him well. He was one of Calvin's cronies. He used to show up when there was a job to be done and not come back until every bullet was spent. He must have been shooting his mouth because he was found with a bullet between his eyes.

I shudder. If I had stayed in Baltimore, it would have been me next. Calvin was never afraid to take out his enemies.

"Excuse me, miss?"

I look up. Thoughts of murdered Pete drop out of my head and disappear like water down a drain.

"Hello."

The man who's interrupted my train of thought is about the most gorgeous creature I've ever seen. He's handsome and clean-cut, wearing neat blue jeans and a crisp, white button-up shirt. He has blond hair that looks like it was due a cut about two weeks ago, but he pushes it back about of his deep blue eyes as he smiles at me.

"I was wondering if you were done with that paper?"

I hurry to fold it up and pass it to him. "I am."

"Thanks." He gestures toward the stool next to mine. "Do you mind if I sit here?"

I move my empty mug out of the way. "Not at all."

I watch him as he pulls up a seat next to me. When he moves past me to step up onto the stool, I catch a breath of his musky, slightly sweet cologne.

"I'm looking for an apartment," he tells me. He spreads the paper out on the counter and flicks to the apartment leases. "I'm new to town."

I bite down on my lip. It excites me to think that this phenomenon of a man with his toned body and killer smile might be here to stay.

Snap out of it, Megan. You should kick yourself for thinking about a man that way for even a second.

"What brings you here?" I ask.

"Luck."

"Luck?"

"Or fate, or chance, or whatever you want to call it." He looks up and smiles at me again. I'm glad I'm sitting down because I'm sure my knees would have grown weak. "It was time for a fresh start. So, I picked up a map of the states, closed my eyes, and my finger landed where it landed. Galena, Illinois."

"You came all the way here because you shut your eyes and pointed?"

"That's right." He laughs. "You must think I'm insane."

"A little."

He shrugs. "There was nothing left for me back in Montana."

"What happened?"

"Love happened." He leans on the counter with one elbow and meets my eye. His eyes are the darkest blue I've ever seen, deeper than sapphires. "My partner of ten years decided she wanted out. Rather than fight over the house and the furniture and all the rest of it, I just walked away. My only regret is leaving the dog behind."

"I'm sorry."

"Don't be. I don't want to spend my life with someone who doesn't want me back." He tilts his head slightly to one side with interest. "What about you? Have you always lived in Illinois?"

"For the last few years."

"Really?"

"Yes. I came for college then just stayed."

"Wow. College. What did you study?"

Lies. Lies. Lies.

I'm well-versed in my cover story. I have to stick to it, but it feels strange to lie so blatantly and extensively to someone's face. Then again, it's liberating too. Instead of saying *I lived with a gangster since I was eighteen, pretending I never noticed the bloodstains in the sink after he beat someone half to death*, I can talk about the catering course I never took. Instead of talking about bloodshed and gunshots, I can talk about historic landmarks and what's best at the café.

"Catering."

I relax into the conversation, even though five minutes ago I was on edge, terrified that someone was speaking to me. I thought I wouldn't be able to stick to the tale, but the lies flow like honey off my tongue.

"What's your name?" he asks me.

I hold out my hand. "Tammy Miller."

JACK

I KNOW her name isn't Tammy Miller. According to the dossier I was given by Sparky after it had gone through enough pairs of hands to meet the three degrees of separation rule, this woman is Megan Cartwright.

She looks just like the picture I had of her, except instead of the long, wavy chestnut hair she had in the photograph, her hair is a straight, blonde and shoulder-length. She's prettier than her picture, also, or maybe she just looks that way because she's out of Baltimore. Skin which looked pale and drawn in the picture is rosy and fresh in person. There are no dark circles under her eyes.

Megan reaches for her second coffee, and I see the little floral tattoo on her inner wrist which I read about, too.

This woman doesn't look anything like I imagined she would. Sparky made out that she was a villainous, cold-blooded criminal with murderous intentions. She looks like a sweet, innocent preschool teacher in her pink cashmere sweater and light blue jeans, a pair of floral flats on her feet. Her make-up is soft and feminine. She looks about as sheltered and innocent as any woman I've met.

"Tammy. That's a nice name. I'm Mark."

She reaches out to shake my hand. As my fingers close around hers, I already know I'm not going to be pulling the trigger of the revolver tucked into the back of my waistband. There will not be a drop of blood on that cashmere sweater or in that blonde hair. Megan Cartwright will be alive when I leave here.

"Do you live alone, Tammy?"

She pauses like an actress with stage fright. Then she remembers her lines. "I live next door to a close friend, so it's not like I'm ever really on my own."

I wonder if WITSEC fed her that one to make sure nobody ever realized how easy it was to get to her.

I could sneak into her house and slit her throat in her sleep.

My blood runs cold at the thought. More than ever, I am certain—*I am not a killer.*

"I might have to get a housemate before I can afford a place of my own." I respond to a lie with a lie of my own. "It might be a while before I find work."

She smiles. "You'll find something. Look at you, you're dressed about as smart as any man I've ever seen. You'd fit right into an office somewhere."

My chest tightens. *Is a change of clothes all it takes for someone to think I might be worth something?*

I lean forward and take a closer look at Megan Cartwright. She's got a soft, sweet face. Her eyes are large and brown. There's a shine behind them where I expected to see the dullness of someone who's killed before; eyes like mine.

Her lips are a soft pink, the teeth beneath them straight and white. When she smiles, it emphasizes her high cheekbones. She's more than pretty. She's beautiful.

When I was first in prison, I thought about women often. I missed them. I longed for them. As the years rolled by, I put thoughts of them to the back of my mind, pushing down those raw desires and fantasies of having a woman's legs wrapped around me, knowing there were many more years to go. I repressed those urges throughout my incarceration, even after when Sparky offered to take me to a strip bar. I haven't thought about a woman's touch in a very long time.

Yet, sitting here next to Megan, I feel a stirring. Primal urges are rising to the surface. I want to take her by the hand, lead her to the nearest bed, have my way with her, then send her safely on her way to some new town where her ex-lover won't find her.

Imagine the thrill of fucking Megan Cartwright, the gang lord's girl.

My mouth grows dry and I swallow, then clear my throat. This is getting dangerous. I put a target on my head the second I decided I wasn't going to go through with this. I'm now in debt to a criminal who paid my airfare and car rental, as well as having failed the task he sent me here to do. I've broken parole with the intent of carrying out an assassination. I've fucked myself by even thinking about taking this path for a moment. And now I'm going to have to live with the consequences of having kept some shred of morality through the years of violence and depravity I've survived until now.

The only thing that could make this worse would be taking Megan Cartwright to bed.

All I can do is walk away, tell Sparky I'm out and hope that those three degrees of separation don't leave me with a knife in my neck. More likely than not, I'll have to disappear from Baltimore to be safe. That means breaking parole and breaking it for good.

You stupid bastard.

Megan bows her head to look into my eyes. "Are you alright, Mark?"

"I'm fine." I force a smile. "I didn't realize that was the time. I've got to go. There's a job fair on today."

She perks up. "Maybe I could come with you."

"It's for IT only. You're a caterer, aren't you?"

"That's right."

She sounds disappointed. I want to tell her she should be thanking God I'm walking away. I have a feeling someone much worse than me is coming.

I fold up the newspaper and slide it back across to her, stepping down from my stool.

"Look after yourself, Tammy."

"You too." She bites down on her lip. "Maybe I'll catch you here again sometime."

"Maybe."

I turn away and leave the café. I'm breathing like I've run a marathon, adrenaline pumping through my veins. I've just sat and had a conversation with a dead woman walking; this time next week, someone will have put an end to her. I walk away knowing that I've achieved nothing by letting her live. I may have my conscience intact, but I've lost $150K, a friend, the only place I had to stay, and a clean parole record.

I've thrown my life away for a woman I'll never know.

And I haven't even saved her.

MEGAN

KHOSA IS DRESSED in what I think is meant to be casual wear, but he can't help standing like an agent of the law. His back is incredibly straight, his shoulders rolled back, his jet-black hair perfectly groomed.

He accepts a cup of coffee and sits across from me on one of the dusky pink suede armchairs that sits opposite my floral-pattern beige-and-pink sofa.

"How are you doing, Tammy?"

I smile. "You know my real name, Inspector Khosa."

"Perhaps, but you need to let it go. It's best we all embrace your new identity."

"I'm surprised to see you here. I wasn't expecting anyone to be checking in so soon."

"Eyes have been on you. You think we'd just drop you off here and then disappear for good? You are being protected, Tammy."

I smile. "Thank you."

Nothing could have jarred me out of the fantasy of a new life quite like a federal marshal sitting in a chair when I came home. It brings everything back to me—the horrible things I have seen and endured, Calvin, the court case, the fact that I'm not free but in hiding; the knowledge that Tammy Miller exists only to keep Megan Cartwright alive.

"How are you settling in here?"

"You know." I fall silent. What is there to say? "I don't really know what to do with myself. I'm hoping to hear back on one of the jobs I've applied for soon. At least then I can get a bit of routine, meet a few new people."

"Have you been going through the persona profile I gave you?"

"Daily."

"Good. That's good. You need to be sure on your story."

"I know."

"And have you had any contact with anyone back home?"

"None."

"Excellent." Khosa smiles. "Then you have nothing to worry about."

"Are you sure?" I reach under the coffee table and pick out the newspaper I saved from last week. I open to the headline story and slide it across to Khosa. "Pete Hetcliffe. Gunshot to the forehead."

Khosa clenches his jaw and gives the paper no more than a cursory glance. Clearly, he's not unfamiliar with the story. "Yes. We're aware of Peter's death."

"Calvin got to him, didn't he?"

"That's what we're inclined to believe. Yes."

"What happened? Did Pete sell him out?"

"Hetcliffe signed an immunity deal; his testimony in exchange for no charges against him. Word got out."

"It seems word keeps getting out. Isn't that why I'm here?"

Khosa clears his throat. "Taking you into witness protection was us being overly cautious."

"No, it wasn't. You know what Calvin is capable of. Just as I do."

"Are you getting cold feet about giving testimony?"

I feel my eyes glazing over into a thousand-yard stare. I let out a long breath, then shake my head slowly. "He needs to go away for the things he's done. Aiden's death opened my eyes. It's one thing to pretend you don't see when it's gangsters killing each other, but another thing when he starts shooting kids."

Khosa reaches over and places his hand on mine. His eyes hold onto my gaze intently. "I won't let anybody hurt you, Megan."

My eyes widen slightly. I get the feeling that Khosa is more than professionally invested in this case. Since I've met him, I've noticed how his gaze has always lingered longer than the other agent's, and how he makes sure he's there at every step of the process. I think he's got a soft spot for me.

I pull my hand away. "You'd best call me Tammy."

"You're right. Of course."

Khosa retracts his hand and takes another swig of his coffee out of one of my heart-patterned cups. "These are new."

I offer a small smile. "Shopping passes the time."

"Is the stipend sufficient?"

"Plenty for just me."

"Have you met anybody yet? Started to speak to people?"

"I've been too afraid," I confess. "I play through conversations in my head, practicing how I'd answer questions, what I'd say... I get tongue-tied even in my imagination. I'm a bad liar." I pause and let out a low, self-aware chuckle. "That's not true. I'm a fabulous liar. I've covered for Calvin more times than I care to admit."

My eyes well with tears. I look up at Khosa. "I'm a bad

person, Inspector. I've never hurt people, but I let people get hurt."

"You were scared of what he'd do to you."

"Yes, but even so…I've been a coward, and that cowardice was witness to so many atrocities."

"You're not the first person to have turned a blind eye in the name of self-preservation."

"Immunity…" I spit out the word. "I don't deserve to escape the jury. I deserve to be judged."

Khosa smiles kindly at me. "You're too hard on yourself, Tammy. You were a prisoner; maybe not behind a locked door, or trapped in chains, but psychologically, he had you in a cage."

"I can't forgive myself that easily. I have to take some responsibility for the things I let happen."

"Enough of that now," Khosa says. "This is a fresh start, and you should treat it as such. If you want to redeem yourself or atone or make good any sense of guilt you're carrying around with you inside, then now's your chance. Volunteer. Advocate. Be kind. You've got a whole life ahead of you to walk a very different path."

I smile. "I will. I've vowed that to myself. From now on, I'm going to be the woman I might have been if I had never met Calvin Raynor."

I brush away the few stray tears that have tracked their way down my cheeks and force a more grateful smile for the marshal.

"I think you'll do very well here," Khosa predicts. "I like to see that you're making this place your own." He picks up a penguin plate full of loose change on my coffee table and smiles. "You weren't you when you were with Calvin. Look at how sweet a home you're making here. I can tell you're a good woman, Tammy."

"I'm hoping if I act like one long enough, somehow I'll make it true."

Khosa glances up at the clock. "I'd best be going now. I've got to be back in Maryland this evening."

I stand up to see him out. "Thank you for the visit, Inspector. It was unexpected."

"I won't leave it too long before I'm back. At least one more visit before I return to discuss the trial. The prosecutor has asked me to pass some documents along to you which I'll bring in person next time. I'll also need to discuss with you how we're going to get you safely to the courthouse. But that will be several months from now. The court date hasn't even been set yet. It's bullshit."

He picks up the coat he'd folded neatly over the arm of his chair and shrugs it on. He reaches out to shake my hand. He hesitates like he wants to do more. I do believe the serious and stern Senior Inspector Khosa would hug me if the situation allowed.

Instead, he clears his throat and steps back after I shake his hand. "Take care of yourself, Tammy. Call me if you have any worries at all. I don't care how small a suspicion it is. I'll fly out here if you feel someone gave you a funny look.

"And try to meet some people," he encourages. "We haven't brought you here for you to live like a recluse. Be wary you keep your story straight but don't be afraid to be a part of this society. This is a new life for you. Make it the life you want."

I see Khosa out. After I shut the door behind him, his words continue to ring in my head. I have been living like a recluse, and I've been lonely as hell.

Except for one man...Mark. I only spoke with him briefly. But in that short time, I was part of the world again and living a life I dreamed was over for me. A life where I could speak to someone without guilt or fear, without wondering whether word would get back to Calvin, without feeling watched or judged or frightened.

I picture Mark's handsome, perfect face when I close my eyes. I smile and plan to return to the café the next morning in the hopes of running into him again.

Khosa is right—I need to make this life a life worth living. I didn't escape Calvin just to be miserable somewhere new.

JACK

EVENTUALLY, I'll have to return to Baltimore and face the fact I've backed out of a contract with the wrong person. But first, I'm going to give myself a few more days of walking as a free man; time to figure out what the hell I'm going to do.

Should I even go back at all?

Should I have already returned? I wasn't the one to pay for my travel to Illinois. The government, my parole officer... they probably haven't realized I've left yet. I could return as if nothing has happened without getting caught for breaking parole.

Then again, if I do return, it's not like I'm going to be able to go on living at Sparky's like I hadn't just dropped him in the shit with whoever this mob boss is. That leaves me with nowhere to live and with no alibis.

It's easier to spend a little more time in this in-between place before the anonymous gangster or my parole officer know I've stepped out of line. Right now, I'm invisible and unaccountable. In this moment, nobody knows how badly I've fucked up except me.

The next day, I go back to the café. Where else am I

going to go?

Megan is there. She's wearing a floral tea dress and flat pumps with a pastel yellow cardigan; perfect for the mild May weather. She's sitting at a different table this time, away from the window, half hidden behind a pillar that cuts through the café floor. It's a table for one, but it's about to become a table for two.

I stand a few feet away and wait until she spots me. Her face lights up. Today she looks more made-up than when I last saw her as if she's making an effort for someone. Her shoulder-length blonde hair has been worked into soft curls. She's wearing makeup that's been carefully applied; a pastel pink lipstick and mascara that makes her doe eyes look Disney-esque.

She's occupying herself with reading a book, the leftovers of brunch on a plate in front of her. The three empty mugs suggest she's been there for a while. Waiting for someone, maybe?

As I look at her, it feels like the weight on my shoulders lessens. I don't know why—she's at the center of all my problems right now; yet, she's beautiful and smiling and makes me feel like not everything is as awful as it seems.

This radiant woman has a target on her head, and she's still smiling like there's sunshine inside her. I want to bask in her rays a while before a target gets placed on my head, too.

"Mark!" Megan stands and lifts herself onto tiptoes to kiss me on the cheek like we're old friends. "Back again?"

"I was hoping I'd be able to borrow your paper again." I chuckle at how lame the line sounds once it's out of my mouth. I pull up a chair to sit at her table. "Do you mind?"

She settles back down into her seat and smooths out her skirt. The smile doesn't leave her face. "Not at all." She gestures to the table. "Be my guest. Look, I even have a paper."

"You buy one every day?"

"I like to keep track of what's going on back in my hometown."

"Why look back?" I pick up the paper and shake out the creases. "You're in a gem of a town. Anything going on in the hometown, then?"

"Nothing that I could find in there. Just as well, they only ever publish murders and rapes these days."

"That's not true." I point to a news story on the fifth page. "The President used the word 'covfefe.'"

"Covfefe?" Megan laughs out loud. Her smile grows wider. There's a sparkle of amusement in her eyes. The smile on her face draws a smile from mine. I can't remember the last time I was in the company of someone who knew how to feel joy. I'm thawing in her sunlight.

I've never heard that word before. "What exactly does that mean do you suppose? I haven't got the first freaking idea."

"It must be a typo."

"He could have deleted it, or edited."

"But he left it there." Megan laughs again. "At least he's owning it. Despite the negative press, he does what the hell he wants. Covfefe. Kind of like 'hakuna matata.'"

"I wish I had that kind of confidence when I screwed up."

"You're talking about your ex?" Megan looks across at me playfully. "Screw her and move on."

"Covfefe."

She raises her current cup of coffee, half-empty, like she's making a toast. "Covfefe."

I relax back in the chair. I like this little coffee joint. It's kind of artisan but hasn't taken it too far. There's only one gluten-free option on the entire menu, and they serve their bagels and toast on plates rather than flowerpots and Tonka trucks. But it's got that airy, rustic feel that a lot of these new places have—specials written in fancy calligraphy on graphite chalkboards, plants in oversized teacups covering the walls. One wall that hasn't been decorated is plain brick left bare.

"I like this place," I say aloud.

"Me, too." Megan tucks her hair behind her ear and smiles at me. "It's kind of hipster, but it hasn't gone *too far*, you know?"

"I know exactly what you mean."

Jesus Christ—I have more in common with my would-be assassination target than my cellmate of ten years.

"It's been a while since I've kicked back like this," I say. "What with the break-up and all that, things have been kind of crazy."

"Then I insist you let me treat you to a touching-the-line-but-not-crossing-it cold brew coffee and the best brownie in the USA."

I laugh. "Don't be silly. The gentleman always pays." I reach for my wallet. *Don't spend too much, Jack. You're going to be sleeping in a doorway soon enough.*

Megan pushes my hand and my wallet away. "You're still finding your feet. Consider it a gesture of friendship from someone who was once new to this town, too."

I put my wallet away and feel humbled. I've had one-night stands, but never a relationship; I've never been on a real date. I've bought women drinks in nightclubs, but I've never paid for a date's meal. Now here Megan is paying for my coffee.

It makes me want to see her again so I can buy her dinner. *I may be the scum of the earth, but I want to treat a woman right.*

Megan returns a moment later with our coffees and snacks on a tray. A waitress spots the growing number of empty mugs at the table and clears it for us.

"I've had about...five coffees now?" Megan laughs. "I'm going to be on a caffeine high all day."

"Needing a boost?"

She runs her finger around the edge of the mug. "I just have nowhere else to be, if I'm totally honest."

"You're out of work at the moment?"

I nod. "I thought I'd step out of school straight into my dream catering job, but it's slim pickings out there. I'm kind of taking a hiatus for a while, living on my savings while I figure things out. All my school friends have gone back to their hometowns. It kind of feels like I'm starting from scratch. I've lived here for years, but I feel like a stranger in this town."

"Tell me about it."

"We're kind of in the same boat," Megan says. "I'm glad I bumped into you the other day. I was starting to feel like an alien in this place. A complete outsider."

"Once the ball gets rolling, things will happen fast." I know I'm talking shit. Some psychopath in Baltimore wants this woman dead; she should be running for her life.

But here I am having coffee with her like we're on a date.

"You're sweet, Mark."

I'm anything but sweet. *There's a revolver hidden in the drawer of a motel room that was meant for you.*

Megan takes a bite of her own brownie and lets out a blissful sigh. "Christ, that's good." She looks up at me. "What are your plans for the day?"

"I'm free as a bird."

"Maybe I could show you around a bit."

"Yeah?"

"Yeah. Why not? I've got to get to know people around here again sometime."

I smile. "I'd like that."

"Great." She takes another bite of her brownie, chews, and swallows. "It's a date."

MEGAN

WE LEAVE the café and start walking side by side. I'm feeling like a schoolgirl with a crush. The last time I felt this intoxicating headiness was the first time I laid eyes on Calvin at the age of nineteen. It makes me wary and unsure, but at the same time, that flood of endorphins is a welcome change from constant terror.

I glance up at Mark as we walk. He must be at least six foot two. He towers over my small five-foot-four frame. He walks with a steady, easy stride like he's taking a stroll through a park on a summer's day, his hands in his pockets. I don't have to rush to keep up with him; he slows to my pace.

I examine him more closely as we stroll slowly through the Galena streets. That easy expression seems more strained when he thinks I'm not looking. I notice him constantly clenching and unclenching his jaw, just as he clenches and unclenches his fists in his pockets.

"Something on your mind?"

"Just motels and jobs." He brushes his hand back through his hair. "And I need to get a haircut sometime soon. I feel like a sheepdog."

"I could—" I stop myself from saying *I could cut your hair*. I'm not a hairdresser anymore, and according to Tammy's backstory, I never was. I rephrase. "I'm no hairdresser, but I could give it a go." I shrug casually. "I used to cut my dad's hair when I was a teen. My mom didn't have the eyesight for it."

Mark smiles. "Yeah?"

"Sure. Don't blame me if you end up looking like a troll doll though."

He laughs. "Nothing can be worse than looking like Justin Bieber. I haven't had bangs since I was nineteen, but this cowlick keeps flopping down."

I reach up and brush it back. "I think it looks cute."

I quickly draw my hand away. I didn't mean to get so close so quickly. I just felt compelled to touch that silky, blond hair and better see his deep blue eyes.

Mark doesn't seem to mind. He tries to hide a smile, but I see it there; bashful like a kid. "So, what's this town got to offer, then?" he asks casually. "Where are we going on this grand tour?"

"How do you feel about Ulysses S. Grant?"

"Would you think I'm unpatriotic if I answered 'completely indifferent'?"

I laugh. "He's a pretty big deal around here. Our eighteenth president moved to Galena in 1860 after serving in the Mexican American War and before the Civil War began. He walked these very streets."

"How are you struggling for work? You'd make the perfect tour guide."

"Only because I've heard the tours so many times." I look up at him with a smile. "I've seen all the museums dozens of times. It passes the time. I know more about Grant than any of our other presidents. His life story will be forever scorched in my brain."

"As a complete novice, I feel like I've got no choice but to follow in your footsteps and learn about this hero of the Civil War."

"You really want to learn about Ulysses S. Grant?"

"Absolutely."

I can't tell if he's pulling my leg or deadly serious, so I decide to call his bluff. "Alright, then. We'll start at the Galena and U. S. Grant Museum."

"Perfect."

I nod across the street. "Let's take the bus."

Mark follows me without objection to the bus stop, and we wait for the bus to arrive. When it does, we step on. There are seats available, but we both gravitate toward the center of the bus and take hold of the same pole. Mark places his hand just above mine; I wish he would slide it down a little, maybe clasp his fingers around mine.

Ten minutes later, we arrive outside the museum. It's a red brick building with an impressive double door entrance and a cute little swinging sign on a green post that reads "Galena Museum."

I step off the bus, Mark a step behind. "Here we are."

Mark takes in a deep breath. "I can't wait to learn about Ulysses S. Grant."

"I'm almost positive you're not taking this seriously."

"I am taking this one hundred percent seriously."

Thank God he's not taking this seriously. If there is one thing my life has been missing, it's laughter. Everything has been tense, terrifying and miserable for years. If a man can make me laugh, I'll fall at his feet. *I need this.*

We enter the museum.

I put on my best tour guide voice. "Now sir, would you like to begin with the Gallery of Heroes or Lead mining in the Northwest Region."

"That's a no-brainer. I clearly want to know about how

the Northwest mined lead. It's been something I've always wanted to know."

I take his hand to lead him to the exhibit. I felt like it was the right moment to try my luck—I'm a tour guide, after all; I wouldn't want him wandering astray. Mark's fingers close around mine.

My God, it feels good to hold someone's hand again.

"Did you know that the word 'Galena' actually means lead ore, which is the namesake of this town?"

"You don't say?"

"Mm-hmm." I nod with excessive enthusiasm. "Now if you follow me, you'll see that this museum is home to an *original* 1930s mine shaft. You won't see one of these every day."

Mark bursts out laughing, enough that he puts a hand on his stomach and bends slightly at the waist.

"You really have memorized the tour, haven't you?"

I laugh at myself. "It's actually more interesting than you'd think." I slow down and start wandering around the exhibit as if it's the first time I've been here. "It's nice to know the history of a place. It makes you feel like you're somewhere with roots." I touch one of the old black-and-white photos affectionately. "So many people lived their lives here."

Mark points toward a contraption on the other side of the room; something that looks kind of like a well with a bucket and rope attached to a spool above the hole.

"And what is this, may I ask?"

I stand in front of the contraption with my hands folded knowledgeably across my chest. "Ah yes, the windlass."

"Windlass?"

"Indeed. Used to lift heavy weights; to bring up the rocks from within the mine."

"That is *fascinating*."

I give him a friendly slap on the arm. "You are such a liar."

He laughs. "I'll behave. I'm interested, honestly."

After that, we begin to really look at the exhibits—from the Driftless Area and First Peoples to Grant's Leather Store, from Galena in Maps to the Vicksburg Flag. We talk. We talk about the past of Galena and our own messy presents—I'm careful not to let any Megan slip out into Tammy's backstory.

That doesn't mean I don't show my own personality at all. I talk about how I loved country music as a teen but refused to ever let anyone find out—I haven't listened to it in years. I tell him about my irrational fear of papercuts, and how I always wear a thimble on my finger when I read to protect myself.

He tells me about his dream vacation to New Zealand, based on his long-term love of Lord of the Rings and about how he swears he predicted VR long before it became a thing.

It's easy, fun, pleasant conversation. Within hours, I feel like I've known Mark a lifetime. I don't let go of his hand while we're walking around, and he doesn't let go of mine either.

I'd planned a whole tour for him, but we end up spending so much time in the museum, that it's five p.m. by the time we get out.

"I'm sorry," I say. "Everywhere will be closing by now."

"That's okay. The lead mining was at the top of my list anyway." His smile softens, and he gives my hand a squeeze. "At least it means I've got a reason to see you again. You've still got so much left to show me."

JACK

WHAT THE HELL is wrong with you, Jack?

Maybe my time in the joint has made my head go soft because I'm acting like a teenager with a crush instead of a convict who's broken a vow. While I was walking around with Megan, the assassination, prison, parole...none of it could have been any further from my mind. She made me forget about everything.

It's an impossible miracle, but true. Today, I felt like an ordinary man with hope for a good life.

Except it's all a lie.

Fuck it. I deserve some shred of happiness before it all comes crashing down again. When will it be my turn to taste the sweet side of life, if not today? I didn't get the chance when I was a kid getting knocked around by Donnie. I didn't get it when I spent fourteen years behind bars, and I sure as hell won't be tasting anything but blood when this gangster finds out who I am. *It's now or never, Jack.*

We're taking the long way back toward Megan's place today. Neither of us wants to cut the date short by taking the bus, so we stroll, hand in hand.

Maybe I'd feel guiltier about lying about who I was if I didn't know that Tammy Miller was Megan Cartwright. It doesn't matter—whoever she is, she's having the strangest and most addictive effect on me. I want her more with each passing moment.

"There's a pizza place over there. Fancy a pie?" I have to prolong our time together.

"I thought you'd never ask. I'm starving."

"My treat."

There I go again, spending money I don't have, making moves on a girl I can't have, living a life that will never be mine. I'm in a fantasy world and digging my heels in to try and stay there just a little longer.

We step into the little pizza joint. It's a dive, but it smells insanely good.

"What's your poison?" I ask her, looking up at the board with dozens of toppings.

"Ham and pineapple, for sure."

"Just when I was starting to like you."

She throws her head back and giggles. "Are you kidding me?"

"I thought we were on the same page, what with our mutual love of mining and former presidents, but this is something I'm going to have to think seriously about if we're going to continue seeing each other."

She grins. "Is that an invitation to another date?"

"Was that a suggestion that this was a date?"

Megan bites down on her lip playfully, sways a little, my hand swinging in hers. She nods. "If it didn't start that way, I hope it's how it ends. I can't remember the last time I enjoyed a day this much."

"Me, either." I smile, feeling that warm fuzzy feeling in my belly that only girls and sissies are supposed to get. Call me a girl or a sissy—I've got man butterflies. "In fact, I enjoyed it so much, I'm even going to allow this *atrocity* to slide." I gesture to get the server's attention. "One large Hawaiian, please." I cast her a sideways glance. "I expect you to eat all my pineapple."

We take our pie and go back outside to find somewhere to eat it. We end up in the parking lot of Sixth Street Baptist Church, sitting on the cold concrete, pizza on our laps out of the cardboard box.

"If I had known this was a date, I would have pulled out more stops," I tell Megan.

She laughs and nestles up against me. The sun is only just starting to set. "I wouldn't change a thing about today."

I look back over my shoulder at the church. The sign of the cross makes me feel instinctively guilty.

Megan follows my gaze. "Are you religious?"

"Not in the slightest."

"Me neither."

"No?"

She makes a face. "There's too much evil in the world."

"My thoughts exactly."

Megan pulls her knees up to her chest. It's like she's shrinking before my eyes, and I know exactly where her mind is taking her. Whoever the man who hired me is, I have no doubt he's evil. *Not like Megan.*

I want to comfort her. I know her time may also be running out, and like me, I want her to have one happy day in this god-damned shitstorm of a life. I put my arm around her and pull her close.

The shadows flee from her face. She closes her eyes, letting out a contented sigh as she lets her head rest against my shoulder.

The hard ground is making my lower back ache. The sour pineapple on the pizza is leaving a bitter taste in my mouth.

I'm wishing I'd brought a jacket now that the sun is going down.

But I wouldn't change a single damn thing. In this moment, I think I might be the happiest I've ever been.

"I don't want today to end," I say.

"What are you talking about?" Megan asks, lifting her head to smile at me. "You've got a haircut appointment at my place tonight."

Who is this woman? She's everything I could have had, everything I didn't know I wanted. I want her now. God knows I want Megan Cartwright.

MEGAN

I HAVE Mark sit down on a chair in front of me and thank God I'd tidied the house that morning. I could almost fool someone into thinking I was usually this neat.

I'm glad he's facing away as I dip a comb into water and comb back his hair. The slightest physical contact with him sends me into a spin; my breathing is coming heavy like I'm an actress in a porno. I have to try and make myself breathe like a normal human being so he won't pick up on how turned on I am just to be touching his delicious, tea-tree scented hair.

"You have beautiful hair," I say. "It's so thick."

Oh God—why did I have to phrase it like that? Now there's something completely different on my mind...

Mark smiles and leans his head back slightly, shutting his eyes. "That feels so good. I'm so relaxed."

"You like it when your hair is combed?"

"I like the way you do it."

I almost start telling him about the autistic child whose hair I used to cut back in Maryland—that sweet but nervous little boy who wouldn't let anyone but me cut his hair—but I can't bring in memories from my past. I'm someone new now.

"I'm trying to be gentle."

I comb his hair far longer than I need to. That tension in his brow is starting to loosen, and I'm enjoying seeing him unwind. I want to move my hands down to his shoulders and massage those taut muscles. I want to run my hands over his chest and massage that too. I want to release the tension in *every* part of his body.

What do you know, Megan? You do still have a sex drive. It was just Calvin's body you couldn't stand anymore.

"I like your place," Mark says. "Very minimal."

I laugh lightly. "When I'm back to work, I'll invest in a few more home touches."

"I used to collect vintage playing cards when I was a teen," he says. "Well, any playing cards that I thought looked old and cool. I had some tobacco ones, some nudie ones—don't judge me—and all kinds of advertising ones. Pre-50s were my favorite. I used to frame them and display them like they were art. That's the only personal touch I ever really invested in. I'm used to bare walls."

"Vintage cards? That's really interesting." I mean it. Mark keeps surprising me with his interests, his sense of humor, his anecdotes. All the people I've hung around for the last decade have nothing to talk about but guns, booze, and sex. I'm fascinated by a man who has an interest as tame as vintage playing cards. It's a breath of fresh air.

"I'd love to see them when you get a new place. Where is all your stuff right now? In storage?"

"My ex has everything," he replies. "I've got nothing to my name."

I put the comb down and run my palms over his hair, pretending to be smoothing off the excess water. Really, I want to offer him some comfort. Poor man—he's had to leave his whole life behind too.

"You can't get it back?"

"It was another lifetime. A fresh start."

I pick up my scissors. "What look are we going for?"

"You're the professional. I'm leaving myself in your capable hands."

My heart skips a beat when he calls me a professional. I question whether he knows who I really am; then I look down at his content, relaxed face waiting for my touch, and I know he doesn't know a thing. It was an innocent, throwaway comment.

Don't be so jumpy, Megan. You're states away from Calvin now.

"The fashion these days is long on top and short at the sides."

"So, hipster but not going *too far* with it?"

I laugh. "Exactly."

I love the way Mark knows how to keep a joke running. After one day together, we already have all these little inside jokes. It's making me feel like he's been here the whole time, like I've known him forever. I know without a doubt, that if he left right now, I'd miss him. He's filling an empty space that's been hollow all my life. I've felt more myself today than ever before.

This is the person I want to be. Museums and haircuts, buses and pizza—an ordinary life.

Fuck it. I deserve to be happy. If I don't chase happiness when it falls into my lap, when will I ever find it? I've done wrong in my life, but I'm making up for it. I want Mark...and I think he wants me too.

I swallow and squeeze my legs together. I'm getting turned on and haven't even started cutting his hair yet.

I pick up a strand of his hair and hold it in place with two fingers, slicing through the hair and letting it drop to the floor. Then I'm on fire, cutting and snipping until I can see a style forming. It feels good to be doing what I do again. I know I'll never get to cut hair again—it was never a big dream, but it was mine. The only thing I ever saw through to the end. I was good at it, people liked me. I miss it.

When I'm nearly done, I grab my dryer and blow dry his hair into place.

"All done."

I hand Mark a mirror, and he examines his own reflection. I see the admiration in his eyes. "Jesus, Tammy. You're good at this."

I beam, then take the mirror to show him the back. "You like it?"

"I think I'm ready to start hitting the street with my resume again. I look like a CEO."

He runs his hand through his hair with a big, cheesy grin on his face, then stands up and turns to face me. I just about melt when he gives me a hug.

"You're a natural. Maybe you should have done hairdressing instead of catering."

He'll never know.

As I'm brushing up the hair from the floor, I notice Mark rubbing at his neck and shoulders.

"I'm sorry," I say, "I should have put a towel around your shoulders. I bet you're covered in stubble."

"That's okay. A small price to pay for a cut this good."

"Do you want to take a shower?"

"Here?"

"I'll run your top through the wash quickly—there's a quick rinse option. Same on the dryer. I can have it washed and dried in the hour."

He pauses. I feel like an idiot for suggesting it. *How strong can you come on, Megan? He probably thinks you're a freak.*

Mark nods. "That would be great. Thanks."

"Okay, then." I jerk my head toward the bathroom. "This way."

He follows me to my small bathroom, which contains a toilet, a tiny little basin and a bath with a glass screen for the shower that hangs on a hook above the tub.

"It's the easiest shower in the world," I tell him. "It runs straight from the tap. Hot is hot, cold is cold. Just flick that one there to turn it on. Chuck your clothes outside the door when you're ready, and I'll stick them in the wash. Toiletries are all there. Use whatever you want."

"Thanks."

I step outside the door and cover my mouth to stop myself squealing as I hop up and down in excitement. Right now, Mark is naked in my house. If it wasn't for the fact I didn't know when he was going to be coming out of the shower, I'd probably be touching myself at the thought.

A few minutes later, I hear Mark calling my name.

I stand on the other side of the door. "Everything okay?"

"Have you got a towel?"

"Oh my god, I'm so sorry." I dart to my bedroom to grab a towel from the linen closet and head back to the bathroom. Keeping my eyes shut and head turned away, I hold the towel through the ajar door.

I gasp slightly when Mark purposefully tugs the towel in such a way as to bring me into the room with it and right into his arms.

The bathroom is steamy, the mirror clouded. The air is humid and filled with the scent of my papaya bodywash. But it's not the steam or humidity that takes my breath away—it's Mark's naked body.

He's staring at me with desire in his eyes, cool as anything. The confidence in the way he stands there, only barely covered by the towel that we're both still holding onto has me weak at the knees.

"Mark..."

Instead of answering, Mark leans forward and kisses me, then pulls back and pauses, waiting for my reaction.

I grab him and pull his face down to mine. I want to kiss him, to taste him. I want him to fuck me in every room in the house. I devour his lips, pressing my tongue deep into his mouth, still warm from the shower water.

He grunts with desire and presses me against the bathroom wall. The tiles make me gasp; they're cold against my skin. I look down. Mark's cock is huge and hard, so big it instantly makes me wet.

Both his arms are covered in grayscale tattoos, but I don't absorb the images. The surprise of the artwork on his body only turns me on more. *There's a naughty boy under that clean shirt.*

Mark takes my dress off over my head in one pull so I'm just in my underwear. I wasn't expecting this. They don't match. I'm wearing an old gray T-shirt bra and pink cotton panties. I don't think Mark notices; his eyes ravage my body, and he moans in approval.

"Jesus Christ, Tammy—you're a bombshell."

"I've been fantasizing about this all day," I confess. My voice is breathless and sultry—it hardly sounds like me, but I love how sexy I sound. I can hear the desperation in my own voice—desperate to be taken. "Do you have a condom?"

"Hang on a second." Mark disappears—presumably to his wallet on the kitchen counter—and returns a second later, already tearing the foil off the condom with his teeth. He spits out the edge, throws the wrapper to the floor and slides the latex down his thick cock.

I'm still standing there with my back against the wall. Mark rests his hand on the tiles above my head, pushing his hand down my panties and slipping a finger inside me. He rubs slowly against my clit. His mouth turns upward into a knowing smile.

"You're soaking wet."

I whimper in desire and do the only thing that's left to do —I take him in my hand. Jesus—he's hard. I swallow past the lump in my throat and start moving my hand up and down his cock. He grows even harder.

Mark's as desperate as I am. As I stroke him, he unclasps my bra and drops it to the ground, kicking it under the tub. His thumbs roll over my nipples, and a sensation jolts through me with each touch. Soon he trails his hands down my sides as he leans forward, taking one of my breasts in his mouth. My nipples harden as he swirls his tongue around my nipple, then bites and sucks. I moan and arch my back as the delicious feeling makes my pussy twitch.

He grabs my wrists and puts my arms above my head and against the wall. "Keep them there." His voice is strong and commanding. "I want to pleasure you."

My body shudders in anticipation. His hands are on my hips now. Lightly he caresses my soft skin along the edge of my panties. A groan escapes his lips as he makes his way down, trailing kisses along my stomach.

"You are so damn beautiful." His breath is hot on my skin, his kisses bringing my desire to new heights.

He gets down on his knees. His strong hands hold me firmly in place as my hips move, wanting more. I keep my arms above my head, stretching my body to increase the tension. When his hot breath reaches lower, he pulls my panties down slowly, his tongue licking along the newly exposed skin.

My pussy aches for him. Aches to feel his fingers and his tongue and his hardness. I feel admired and adored and so hot.

He pulls my panties down to my knees and I kick them

away too. He looks down to my exposed pussy and lets out a breathy moan of approval.

He dives in with his tongue, sliding along my folds and making circles around my button. I cry out in pleasure. His mouth is on me, his tongue penetrating inside while he pushes his finger inside me. The muscles of my vagina clench, begging for more. He moves just right, his finger sliding in and out of me, making me crazy. I begin to fuck his hand as he speeds up the motions, finger fucking me while his thumb rolls over my button.

He moves his mouth to my breast and flicks my nipple at the same time he flicks my clit with his thumb. The combination of the two sends my arousal speeding toward an orgasm. My body is stretched against the tile, legs shaking and hips moving. I feel my orgasm wind around me.

I'm almost there, teetering on the edge of a cliff when he stops. He steps back, leaving me there panting and moaning. My eyes get wide, and he stands over me, looking at my half naked body moving as if he were still pleasuring me.

"Mark, I need you." My voice is breathy and pleading.

The humidity and steam are making my hair damp. My skin is clammy with steam and sweat. I can feel the perspiration on my breasts. Mark grabs me by the waist and spins me around.

I plant my hands on the tiles and lean forward, standing on my tiptoes and lifting my ass so I'm the right height for him to enter me. He groans as his cock slides inside. I gasp at the feeling of my pussy opening to receive him. He hesitates, only moving slightly back and forth. The feeling teases me and makes me crazy with lust. I push back, but he follows me.

I whimper, desire overwhelming my senses.

"You feel so fucking good." He bites at the back of my neck.

Then he presses hard and deep, making my chest press against the cold tiles.

I'm hot and cold and sweaty and gloriously dizzy, drowning in the scent of papaya and the feeling of being so aroused I might pass out. I push my hips back into Mark. I want him deeper, faster.

He reaches around and massages my breast as he pounds into me. Looking over my shoulder behind me, I see him biting down on his lip; his expression a sensual blend of focus and pleasure.

My feet are slipping on the floor. I press myself closer to the wall to keep my balance. My legs are stretched with trying to stay tall enough for Mark to fuck me.

He places his lips next to my ear. I can hear his heavy breathing; it makes me wetter.

"The bedroom," he growls.

He steps back, and I take his hand to drag him after me into my bedroom. The bed isn't made and the drapes are open, but we're not going to stop over small details.

I drop back onto the bed, relishing the chance I have to look at Mark in all his glory—ripped, erect, and hot as hell. He strides over to me and pounces onto the bed, bouncing slightly as he lands on the mattress.

He throws my left leg over his shoulder and lowers his body to fuck me. The position is incredible; I can feel every inch of him inside me. My toes curl in the air as he rocks into me.

"Touch yourself."

I do as Mark says and reach down between my legs to rub my own clit. Within seconds, I'm gasping. I'm so wet, it takes nothing but the slightest touch to turn that tingle into electricity. I arch my back in pleasure and moan.

That spurs Mark on. He moves faster, deeper. I come,

crying out and letting my hands fall above my head, my hands curling into fists as I squeeze my eyes shut and gasp.

"That's it," he murmurs. "Be as loud as you want."

My leg drops down. Mark grabs my hips and moves faster and deeper. He starts to grunt as he gets closer to his own release—and then it comes. He moans as he explodes inside me, then lowers his body atop mine, to catch his breath.

He lifts his upper body to look into my eyes. He smiles and strokes my hair. "Wow, Tammy. You're a goddess."

I laugh. *Am I the one who should be getting praised here?* "You're not too bad yourself."

"It's crazy the kind of confidence a good haircut gives a man."

I laugh, catch Mark's eye, and start laughing more. I'm dizzy with the elation of incredible sex and incredible company.

This has been the best day of my life.

Fuck it—I don't care if it's been five minutes.

I'm in love with this man.

JACK

I CAN'T STAY HERE in Galena forever acting like nothing's wrong.

Soon, they're going to send someone else for Megan, and I can't let anyone hurt her. I think I'm in love with this woman.

Call me crazy, I don't care. I've known a lot of hate and even worse—indifference—in my life, but nothing like this. I came here to kill Megan, but god knows I'd die for her now.

I've made up my mind. I'm going to make sure Megan leaves this place. In the meantime, I'm going to go back to Baltimore to get a read from Sparky on what Calvin's planning on doing next.

I have Megan's number now, and she has mine. If she gets relocated by witness protection, maybe she'll never contact me again—as any sensible woman would do. But maybe, if she feels the same electricity I do, she'll break the rules to see me again. That's all I can hope for now.

I get up and get dressed.

Megan looks confused. She sits up in bed and tilts her head to one side. "Where are you going."

"I'm so sorry, Tammy. I didn't know I'd be staying this long. I've got a flight to catch tonight."

"Where are you going?"

"Montana."

"Why?"

"I've got some things to settle up with my ex. I don't want to go," I kneel one knee on the mattress and lean across the bed to kiss Megan, "but the sooner I get it done, the sooner I can move on. I'm going to rip off the band-aid now. I want that woman out of my life so I can start afresh."

Megan hugs her knees. She looks disheartened. "I forgot about her. Maybe we took things too fast."

I sit down beside her and turn her face toward me. "No, Tammy. No way. If anything, you've made me realize how much time I've wasted with the wrong person. Today was...*everything*. I want to cut all ties with everything I was before. I don't think choosing Galena happened by chance. I think life was finally pushing me toward the person I'm meant to be with."

She laughs uncertainly. "Mark! We've only been on one date."

"You're right. I'm sorry. I sound insane."

Megan reaches out to place her hand atop mine. "Go do what you need to do. I'll plan the next tour."

"Really?"

"Today was everything to me too."

My little speech was bullshit, but the sentiment wasn't. I really do believe fate led me to Galena for a reason. I'm meant to save Megan Cartwright. Some divine force is proving to me that I'm not the evil monster the world thinks I am or that I almost became. Life is giving me another chance to redeem myself, to love and be loved.

I'm going to go back to Baltimore and cut ties with Sparky and my old life. I'm going to write to my parole officer and tell him I'm sorry—I couldn't stay in Baltimore. Then I'm going to leave the cleanest, most honest life I can wherever Megan ends up—after I do what I have to do next.

* * *

I know I'm going to scare Megan, but it's for her own protection. She can't stay in Galena—but I can't come clean.

This anonymous warning is all I can do. I wrote it back in the motel room, getting the words on paper before I checked out.

Megan Cartwright. I know who you are and where you live. I'm going to kill you, bitch. You can't run, you can't hide.

I felt disgusted as I wrote the words and sick when I pushed the envelope through Megan's mail slot and sprinted down the street before she saw me.

She's going to open it and be terrified, but I had to make her realize she's in danger. Now she'll call the feds, and they'll relocate her. Calvin won't know where she is. She'll be safe.

I might never see her again, but I'll suffer a broken heart to save her.

I'm sorry, Megan. I know our day was everything.

MEGAN

MEGAN CARTWRIGHT. I know who you are and where you live. I'm going to kill you, bitch. You can't run, you can't hide.

I can't breathe. My throat has closed up and I'm gasping, clutching my chest as I hyperventilate and suffocate at the same time. I fall down into my seat and reach for my cell.

I have to call Khosa—now.

I find him in my contacts and go to press 'dial.' Then—I stop.

If I call Khosa, I'll be relocated and never see Mark again.

Don't be stupid, Megan. You'd risk your life for a man you just met? For a relationship that might never happen? For someone you hardly know?

The thought of never seeing him again is more than I can bear. In the shortest time imaginable, Mark has come to mean so much. He's the hope I've been waiting for; he's the better life I dream about. Without him, I'm just Megan Cartwright in disguise. With him, I'm Megan Cartwright: free and truly seen.

I've never laughed the way I've laughed with him. I've

never felt so open the way I've felt with him. I've never made love the way I made love to him.

It's only the relief of being away from Calvin. You're just too scared to be alone.

No, that's not true. I know it's not true.

The only thing I'm scared about is having done all this only to be left with a fragment of a life, a shadow of a real happy ending. I want the fairytale happily ever after. I want my Prince Charming. I want Mark.

I've been beaten and silenced, degraded and abused. I've witnessed torture, murder, and unimaginable violence. I've hidden behind locked bathroom doors, in fear for my life. I've tolerated the company of sick, disturbed men. I turned against the most powerful and dangerous man in Baltimore.

And only half of the reason I came forward was because of Aiden. The other part of me was simply sick of living a bullshit charade of a life.

I can't do it all again.

I'm not strong enough, and I'm not willing.

I want Mark. I want love. I want happiness. I want jokes in museums, Hawaiian pizza, and mind-blowing sex. I want holding hands and bus rides and an arm around me.

Swallowing back my fear and taking deep breaths until my tears dry up without falling, I crumple the note in my hand and throw it in the wastebasket.

Come at me, motherfucker. I'm living for me now. Tell Calvin he can go fuck himself.

JACK

I DRAG out the walk back from the train station as long as I can. Nothing's waiting for me in Baltimore but bad news. Still, eventually the sidewalk runs out, and I'm standing outside Sparky's. I wouldn't have come here at all if every single thing I owned wasn't in a bag in his living room.

I don't need to unlock the door. As always, it's open. I push it in and try to creep toward my belongings without making a sound.

"Strike?"

I wince. "Yup."

Sparky races down the stairs, his feet pounding down the creaking steps. He appears at the doorway looking wired, his eyes wide. He punctuates his speech with deep, loud sniffs like there's a little something still left in his nose from some kind of party the night before. He drags the back of his hand across his nostrils.

"You've been gone for days. I thought you'd done a runner on me." He laughs maniacally. "Good thing you're not that dumb. So?" He grins. "You got it done?"

I pick up my bag and sling it over my shoulder. "No."

"What do you mean 'no'?"

"I couldn't do it."

Sparky falls silent. He rolls his tongue around his teeth and breathes in deeply through his nostrils, making a long, drawn-out snorting sound. He clears his throat. "You couldn't do it?"

"Nah, man."

"That's the best you've got?" His voice rises. "You waltz in here like that's good enough? What was it? Feds were watching? Gun jammed? Your fucking balls dropped off?"

"She's just a regular girl, Sparky. She doesn't deserve a shot in the head from a stranger."

"For fuck's sake—do you have any idea what kind of shit you've dropped me in?" He sweeps his hand across the table against the back door and sends a row of bottles crashing to the ground. "I stuck my neck out for you."

"I told you I wasn't interested."

"You said you would do it."

"Well, I didn't."

Sparky punches the wall. My heartbeat fastens as I watch him lose his temper. I know Sparky's not the most stable of guys, and I know he keeps a revolver in the cabinet drawer just a few steps away.

"I'm sorry. I got there. After I met her, I knew I couldn't do it. Jesus, even if it wasn't her...I couldn't kill anyone. That's not who I am."

"It is who you are. How else do you explain the ten years we shared a cell? Not that the time meant shit to you anyway. You've thrown me under the bus with this bullshit."

"I'll pay the guy back for the travel as soon as I can."

"That's the least of your worries. You've let down a dangerous man."

"Yeah? And exactly who is this guy? This big boss man who hasn't got the guts to do his dirty work himself? If he wants to hunt down his ex, that's his problem. I'm not pulling the trigger to tie up someone else's loose ends."

"Fuck you, Jack."

I hold up my hands. "I'm out of here."

"Take your shit with you. I'm not your meal ticket or your storage unit. You're on your own now, man. Completely on your own."

I pound up the stairs to grab my cell charger and the couple of toiletries I have left in the bathroom. I turn around to go back downstairs when I spot the medicine cabinet, and a vengeful feeling rises up in me.

I peer down the stairs to judge if Sparky is about to come up. I can hear him slamming things around downstairs. He's talking to someone on his cell, telling the story of how I fucked up the hit. I can hear him screaming on the line.

"I know, I know. We're both in deep shit, Micky. Now I've got to find some other guy to do the job, and my network ain't that wide, you know? I wouldn't have jumped on it so fast if I wasn't so sure Strike was going to pull through for me. Fucking pussy couldn't pull the trigger, and now I've got to find someone else to kill that bitch."

My stomach sinks. Just as I suspected, nothing's changed. Sparky's still going to find someone else to finish the job.

Please God, Megan—take that note seriously and get out of town.

I go to the medicine cabinet and open the door. The cabinet is built into the wall, and I know there's a secret compartment under the bottom shelf. After quickly and quietly moving the items, I pull up the shelf. I reach into the compartment to where the envelope is secured by a length of elastic screwed in place.

Sparky told me he had a place to hide all his junk, and I know exactly where that spot is. He'd once told me when he was high that if he ever got taken out, he wanted me to take that envelope and take care of "his guys."

I peer inside the envelope.

Holy shit—there must be a pound of cocaine along with a gun and a wad of cash. I don't feel the slightest guilt at pocketing the money. Sparky owes me for fucking up my life by bringing me into this in the first place. And the last thing I want to do is give him the means to take care of "his guys." Any one of those men might be the next to try and take Megan out.

I go back downstairs and make a show of leaving.

"Shame to leave it this way, Sparky."

"Fuck you."

"I didn't realize our friendship was based on murder."

"It was based on trust, you coward. You broke that trust. You're a traitor." He spits at my feet. "People like us have got to have each other's back because nobody's got ours. You don't understand that."

"People like us?" I let out a bitter laugh. "Sparky, I am nothing like you."

* * *

The waitress offers me a disapproving frown after refilling my coffee for the dozenth time.

"This ain't a motel, you know. You can't just loiter all night."

"The place is dead."

"The diner's for customers only and one cup of coffee only buys you a spot for so long. If you don't order something, I'm going to have to ask you to leave."

"I'll have a piece of pie."

"What type?"

"I don't care."

She bristles at my response but refills my mug and heads

behind the counter to serve me a thick slice of key lime pie from under the large glass display.

I take the opportunity while she's gone to discreetly pull out Sparky's cash and try to find a bill smaller than a hundred. I haven't had a chance to count properly, but I think there's about ten grand in that stack.

I peel a fifty from the load and quickly shove the rest of the cash back in my pocket. I feel smug feeling the weight of it resting against my thigh. *Fuck Sparky*.

The waitress returns with the pie and places it down in front of me with all the grace of a prison warden and then disappears into the kitchen to have a bitching session with the cook.

I sigh and pull out the thirty-dollar cellphone I bought the day after I got out of prison. I'd hoped it would connect me to all the job offers that never came. I'd have settled for an interview, to be fair. But the best—the *only*—offer I had was to be a gunman for some crazed gang lord who liked to give orders via his lackeys.

I scroll through the contacts list as if there would have magically appeared some new names alongside Sparky and my parole officer. I've got nobody to call and nowhere to go. Not now that Megan's moved on.

I picture her in the café, beautiful and looking as sweet and innocent as any woman ever has the very first time I saw her. I recall the smile that never left her face at the museum and the way she looked up at me with endless affection when I told her all the nothing-special things about me, like the way I love Lord of the Rings and vintage cards—all true.

I'd smile at the memory if it didn't seem so distant. I'll never see her again, most likely. If she paid any heed to my note, she'd be on the wind by now. There's no way she could ignore a clear threat like that. WITSEC will be whisking her away as we speak.

At least whoever goes after her now will never find her.

I'm heartbroken it's going to end like this. Megan was the first light to ever shine in my life, but this is for the best. She's safe, and better still, we went our separate ways before she could ever find out I came to kill her. In her mind, I'll always be the guy who was her everything for a day.

My cell buzzes in my hand, and I frown. A shudder runs down my spine. *Is Sparky threatening my life already?*

I open the message. Shock runs through me.

Hey stranger. When are you back in Galena? I've planned a trip to the home of the man himself—Ulysses S. Grant. Maybe this Saturday?

What the hell? I read and re-read the message, checking the number. It's from her cell. But that means she's still in Galena and making plans for the weekend. Did she not get the note? Did WITSEC refuse to rehouse her? Does she not care?

A different shudder runs down my spine; this time it's fear for her.

Megan's in danger, and I'm sitting at a gas station diner drinking cheap coffee and staring at a slice of key lime pie.

I throw the fifty down on the counter and rush out the door. At least now I know where I'm headed—Megan needs me in Illinois.

MEGAN

I SIT in the coffee shop once more for another morning latte and a browse through the paper. No news on Calvin—although, to be honest, in recent days, something else has been drawing me to the café other than the news.

Perched on the stool at the bar by the window, I crane my neck to look down the street. Mark's meeting me here soon. When I texted him about Saturday, he practically bit my hand off, begged me to see him sooner.

I love that. A man who doesn't play games. At least it means he wants to see me as much as I want to see him. Asking to see him on Saturday was my utmost attempt at playing it cool.

I wonder how things have gone back in Montana for him. My stomach turns at the thought of him spending time with his ex. *What if there's a spark when he sees her again? What if I'm a rebound?*

There's more on my mind than worrying about whether I'm Mark's one and only, though. That note has me in a perpetual state of terror. Someone is after me.

I cast my gaze around the café. Maybe it's that older man

over there in the knitted sweater with the crossword puzzle? He's got something of the Wild West about him; maybe he's a secret gunslinger, an expert in assassination.

Or maybe it's the woman in the corner with the black ponytail. Maybe her life of crime started when she poisoned her first husband—a man like Calvin—maybe she got a taste for it; the power.

I shudder. It could be anyone.

"Tammy?"

Mark.

There he is. He's no less gorgeous than the last time I saw him. His sandy blond hair looks neat and modern in the style I cut for him; there's a few days' stubble on his cheeks. He's wearing beige chinos and a pastel blue button-up shirt. He looks like the sort of clean-cut, trustworthy and successful man my mother would have chosen for me. Except I know there are tattoos beneath those sleeves and a beast waiting to come out in the bedroom.

"Mark!" There is genuine delight in my voice. "You're here."

"Am I late?"

"No. I don't know why I sound so surprised. Why wouldn't you come?"

Mark looks stressed. There are dark circles under his eyes, and his actions are short and tense. I guess a run-in with the ex does that.

He pulls up a stool beside me and sits down. His blue eyes look weary and dull, the creases around them deep and heavy.

"How was business with the ex?"

He makes a face. "Not the way I wanted things to end, but what can you do? When someone's decided they hate you, there's nothing you can do."

"I can't believe there's anyone that hates you."

"Anyway, I'm back here now. Thank God."

He smiles and lets his gaze linger on me a while. I feel shy under his stare; nobody's ever looked at me that way before.

"Where are you staying this time?"

"There's a motel on the outskirts of town."

I picture us writhing in motel bedsheets, Mark's hands on my smooth skin. I imagine my hands messing up his neat hair. I picture my legs around his waist; turning a good boy bad.

My face is flushed. I clear my throat and push back my hair behind one burning ear. Memories of our night together are as vivid as if we've just tumbled out of bed.

"I'm sure you'll find somewhere soon."

"I hope so. What about you? How is the job hunt coming?"

"Slow." I shrug. "To be honest, I didn't do any job hunting yesterday."

"Too busy planning the second stage of the Ulysses grand tour?"

I smile. "That's right."

Mark's telling jokes but I can tell his heart isn't in it. It's making me worry. I reach out and place my hand on his arm.

"Are you really alright? Did something happen while you were in Montana?"

"It's just the realization that I've thrown years of my life away and don't have the first idea how to get back on my feet again. I kind of feel like I'm destined to fail. It feels like it's all going to come crashing down." He looks across at me with sorrow in his eyes. "Especially since meeting you. It's too good to be true, you know?"

"I know. I feel the same." I stroke his arm softly, spinning my finger in soft circles against his skin. "But I'd rather be afraid of a good thing than stuck living with the bad things. You've got to take risks to find happiness. You're going to be okay."

"Why is it that I only believe that when I'm with you?"

He speaks to my heart. I feel exactly the same. It's like we're reading from the same script in a story that was written for us. *A love story*.

Mark looks down at his watch. "Have you had breakfast yet?"

"I usually treat coffee as breakfast."

"There's a little bistro place down the street that does a phenomenal brunch. Fancy joining me for a bite? I'm starving."

"I'd love to."

He smiles. "Great."

We finish our coffees and head a couple of blocks over to a bistro I've never been to. As we walk, I'm hyper-aware of how close Mark is to me. I keep shooting glances upward to his handsome face, feeling a secret inner joy that he's near me. After so many years of violence and chaos, I'm drawn to the easy, affable nature of this man. I can't sense any malice in him, and that's something I haven't felt for a long time around the company I've been used to keeping.

"How have you been in general?" I ask him.

"What do you mean?"

"You've not spoken about the break-up. I know that's tough. So...how have you been?"

Mark smiles. "I'm doing okay. You know how it is. You must have had break-ups too. I refuse to believe someone like you has ever been single long."

I nod. Fleeting images of Calvin pass through my mind's eye, inseparable from images of blood, guns, and the feeling of intense panic and fear.

"I was with a man for a very long time, but we'd grown incompatible."

That's a mild way of putting it. Calvin saw his future as a mob boss, and all I wanted to do was get out. He wanted to kill; I wanted the kind of life where the most guilt I'd feel in one day would be over forgetting to defrost the meat for dinner.

We enter the bistro. It's cute, bright and airy inside with glossy wood flooring, abstract art on the walls, and little square wood tables partnered with burnt-orange and gray suede wing chairs.

A waitress soon comes to take our orders.

"Bacon and avocado on toast for me, please," I say. "And an orange juice."

"I'll have the fried chicken biscuits, please." Mark hands back his menu and looks at me with a boyish grin. "I can't get enough of biscuits and gravy."

"My mom used to make them from scratch," I tell him. "The best I've ever had."

"Oh yeah? Maybe I'll have the chance to try some sometime."

My stomach twists in gleeful knots. I can't tell Mark that I haven't spoken to my mom in over ten years or that I never got the chance to learn the recipe from her. He'll never know that I left home at fifteen to follow a dangerous man—because Tammy Miller led a wholesome life. The past I'll tell him about is a lie; a quiet, beautiful lie.

"What about your mom? A good cook?"

He makes a face. "Terrible. The worst."

"Well, I guess not every mother can be a whiz in the kitchen."

"She couldn't cook to save her life. Made a mean Bloody Mary, though."

Mark catches himself and clears his throat. I've touched a nerve mentioning his mother; there's clearly a story there. I heard the resentment in his voice before he stopped talking.

"Do your parents know you're in Galena?" I ask him.

"They know."

"When will they come visit? Maybe we can take them on stage three of the Ulysses S. Grant tour."

Mark shakes his head. "I doubt they'll be visiting any time soon."

"Why not?"

"Let's just say we're estranged."

I have to bite my tongue to stop myself from saying "Me, too." The last words I ever heard my Dad say to me was that I was a reckless slut who was throwing my life away.

You were right, Daddy.

The food arrives, and Mark digs in. The way he eats makes me smile—like he's savoring every mouthful. He even shuts his eyes at one point and lets out a low moan. He's surprised when I laugh.

"What?"

"You're enjoying those biscuits."

He wipes his mouth with a napkin and chuckles. "I've been living on vending machine snacks for a few nights."

"I'm not a bad cook, you know. You should come around for a home-cooked dinner one night. You can use my laptop to look for apartments."

"Yeah?" He pauses mid-bite, then smiles. "That'd be nice."

I beam. I've finally made a connection with someone. When Witness Protection first came for me, I felt like I was making a trade-off—loneliness for safety. It was a trade I'd make a hundred times over, but that didn't make me any less sorrowful when I spent day after day in a new apartment on my own.

"So, tell me more about this town I'm moving into. How are you enjoying Galena?" Mark asks me. "You're brave being here on your own."

I shrug. "It's the cost of going your own way."

"Do you have visitors? You know, people who are looking out for you?"

I think of Khosa, the only man who has my back, but I can hardly bring him into the conversation. I offer a wry smile. "My family will visit soon." *Tammy's fake family*.

"Must be tough, being alone. Do you get scared?"

I laugh nervously. "Should I be?"

"Of course not. I know some girls get funny about living alone though. I used to have a friend who'd call me every time the wind blew, thinking it was someone trying to break in. Do you ever get that? The feeling like someone's watching you?"

I close my fingers tightly around my cutlery and lean back a little in my chair. Mark's hitting a little close to home, and it's making me suspicious. I examine his face; his expression is neutral and shows no sign of any kind of understanding of why his words might have sent chills down my spine. I make a conscious effort to relax my shoulders.

"Never."

"Then you'll be fine." He smiles. "You're clearly made of tougher stuff."

"Why? Do you get creeped out by the wind in the motel?"

"Not the wind, no. But a couple were having some nasty sex last night."

The change in topic catches me by surprise, and I let out a gasp of laughter. "Loud, were they?"

"Not just loud, but *descriptive*." He mimes holding onto a woman's hips and moans an impersonation. "Keep going. Deeper, deeper. No, not like that. To the left, to the left, *faster*. Did the condom just fall off?"

I laugh so hard I get some orange juice caught in the back of my throat and start to splutter. Mark hands me a napkin so I can wipe my nose.

"That sounds horrendous."

"It wouldn't be so bad it the headboard of their bed didn't

back onto my wall. I spent the night dreaming there was a ram trying to escape from its enclosure."

He's funny. I bite down on my smile, finding myself enjoying this man's company. It's good to laugh. In fact, I can't remember the last time I genuinely laughed. Every time a chuckle has escaped my lips in recent years, it's been an obligatory half-assed sound to stop Calvin getting offended that I didn't find some crude joke about a woman's tits or some racist one-liner funny.

"I think I saw them check out this morning, though, so hopefully I won't have to endure another night of narrated intercourse."

"I remember. You have sex in complete silence."

"Not a word." His eyes sparkle with humor. "I just make really intense eye-contact. But wordlessness is key. Wouldn't want to interrupt the never-ending stare with dialogue."

"Oh no, that would just make it weird. The thing I loved most about our sex was the silence."

"Maybe my wife left me for a more vocal lover."

The smile falls from my face. "I'm sorry."

"Don't be. You've got to move on, right? I'll have to learn to laugh about it sometime."

"Maybe dinner will help?" I suggest. "Tomorrow night?"

"Really?"

"Sure. It sounds like you could do with a night to let your hair down. We can talk about what the hell we're both doing in this dead-end town, and I can give you the pre-tour context for seeing the *very house* that our eighteenth president lived in."

"I thought you said Galena was lovely?"

"It is lovely, in a Hallmark Christmas movie type of way, but I can't see much ever happening here."

"That's not the worst thing in the world. Some places in the world are filled with too much...action. I, for one, am glad to be somewhere where life can slow down a little. You're not thinking of leaving, are you?"

"I doubt it. It took a lot to make it this far. I'm ready to set my roots here. I'll make the most of it." I look at up at him and smile, unashamed of the flirtatious lilt in my voice. "Besides, I've got a feeling this town is about to get a whole lot more interesting."

We finish brunch, then Mark offers to walk me home. *He's such a gentleman.*

I agree, and we head back to my apartment at a slow, easy pace. I let all my worries about Calvin and the trial disappear to the back of my mind while I focus on fantasizing over Mark—not just about the sex, but about what a normal life might look like. Maybe I could end up with him; someone sweet, funny and interesting without a sinister past like Calvin. I've spent a lot of time with Mark now, and I'm still waiting to see that red flag telling me to run a mile.

When we reach my apartment, Mark steps forward, placing his hand on the back of my head and holding my gaze for a moment before kissing me, like he's drinking in the sight of me. The way he stares with this kind of wonder in his eyes makes my heart flutter even more than the kiss. He makes me feel seen and beautiful and interesting. He's the complete opposite of Calvin who made me feel small, repulsive, and invisible.

"Tomorrow night can't come soon enough."

It's my turn to step forward and plant a simple, quick kiss on his lips. The feeling of his stubble on my mouth sends delicious shivers down my spine.

Mark's smiles. Some of that darkness around his eyes dissipates for a moment. "I'll see you tomorrow."

"I can't wait."

JACK

WHILE MEGAN SPUN a world of stories over brunch, I let slip one or two truths that were a little close to home. I think she read the tone of my voice when I mentioned my mom and the Bloody Marys. I had to bring the talk back to fiction by throwing in a comment about the fictional wife who left me for a fictional man over fictional bad sex.

I smile at that last part. Megan had laughed hard when I'd told that story. In fact, that was also true. I've been bedded up in a motel ever since I first left Baltimore to track Megan down, and it seems to be the Illinois headquarters for sloppy midnight sex.

Sparky's been trying to reach me ever since I took off from his place. I've got a dozen furious voicemails about how I've screwed him over and demanding back-rent for the nights I spent at his place. Apparently, he only puts up friends for free.

Nothing about the stolen cash yet, though. I block his number. I've had enough of him. I don't need to hear anything more from my ex-cellmate and the effigy of a real criminal.

I switch off my cell now. I need to be quiet for what I'm about to do next.

I've returned to Megan's apartment. Standing by the porch, I remember the feel of her lips on mine just hours earlier. I liked the way it felt when she came near me without fear and dared to treat me like an ordinary man and not like some killer. More than that—she looks at me the same way I look at her: like she's falling for me.

Maybe this is what life could be like.

I tell myself to stop daydreaming. I've got work to do.

When I left Sparky's a few days earlier, it was with no idea of what the hell I was going to do next. All I knew is that it wasn't safe in Baltimore anymore. I wouldn't put it past Sparky to point the finger at me whenever his mysterious boss was came looking to place the blame on the failed hit, and I didn't want to be around when Sparky came like Judas in the night to turn me in.

I had no plans beyond that. I thought my note would do the trick. I thought Megan would be long gone. But here she is. *Why?*

With nothing to lose, I might as well devote whatever time I have until I'm discovered breaking my parole or caught by the gangster trying to protect her. Someone else will come, and while Megan may not know how to see the signs, I've spent years in the company of murderers and thieves.

It's dark outside. There's a deathly quiet in the air that makes me even more aware of every little sound I make. A single noise that's just a little too loud could draw attention from any one of the dozens of apartment windows over-looking this street. I have to do this quietly.

There's a fire escape on the outside of the building. Looking up at the windows and counting apartments, I figure out which one is Megan's.

I climb the cold iron staircase up to the third story. Looking in through the window, I see the cozy, minimally furnished living room where I sat when she cut my hair. I can still feel her hands stroking back the strands and how relaxed I felt.

I pull the crowbar I bought with me out of the back of my pants and slide the hook under the old wooden windowsill. I press my weight down on the handle and freeze when the wood creaks and sends a loud snapping sound echoing through the night sky.

If I thought I could do this during a date, I would, but there's no time. I need to scope this place out *now* to know whether Megan is already on some murderer's radar.

Instinctively, I crouch down and stay as quiet as possible, waiting to find out if I've been discovered. After three minutes of squatting in the darkness, it seems nobody heard or nobody was suspicious enough to investigate.

I rise to my feet and press down on the crowbar again. The slower I go, the less sound it makes. I wiggle the crowbar side to side, then inch the handle downward, slowly working the stiffness out the panel.

Finally, I'm able to push the window upward and open. I leave the crowbar resting outside against the fire escape handrail and dip down to step over the sill into the living room.

My foot hits the carpet, and I'm grateful for the padding underfoot, disguising the sound of my footsteps. I slowly lower the window back down into place—I don't want any sudden sounds outside to wake Megan before my work is done.

What is my work?

I'm searching for signs this place has been marked, bugged, or targeted in any way. All I knew when I received the documents from Sparky was that Megan Cartwright was in Galena, Illinois and had been spotted at the café by one of the mob boss's spies. If Megan hadn't been sticking to such a rigorous routine, I might never have found her in the first place.

I walk through the apartment in the pitch darkness to the front door. I slide open both deadbolts and ease the door open, running my gloved fingers over the doorframe. I'm searching for any signs of forced entry—such as marks from a crowbar. I want to know if anyone has been here before.

I see no damage and no other signs that Megan's being watched such as symbols on the doorframe. I close the door, lock it once more, and return to the living room.

Item by item, I look underneath, around and inside everything, using a two-dollar flashlight to investigate. I'm looking for wires, recordings, anything suspicious.

Her living room is clear; so is her kitchen and bathroom. There's one room left—the bedroom where she lies sleeping.

I close my hand around the door handle and push it inward. I step in silently. *Maybe I should have taken up burglary instead of manslaughter.* I'm good at this.

Now my eyes have adjusted to the dark, it's easy for me to make out Megan sleeping. Her face is further illuminated by the red light of the numbers of her bedside alarm clock.

She's wearing a gray floral silk nightdress. One of the straps has slipped from her shoulder, exposing her smooth, bare skin. Her shoulder-length blonde hair lies gently against her cheek. Her head is turned to one side, one hand above her head, the other across her stomach.

Despite the imminent danger she is in, she sleeps soundly. *She has no idea the wolves are at the door.*

I watch her for far longer than I need to. I'm hypnotized by her rhythmic, calm breathing and trapped in my own wonderings about this mysterious ex-girlfriend of a distant monster.

What life did you lead before you came here, Megan Cartwright?

I could watch her for hours, but every second I'm here is a risk. I've already broken a contract with a murderous ganglord and broken parole. I'm awaiting my own downfall while I try to save Megan from hers. I need to make the minutes count.

The tour of the bedroom is quick and silent. I pause only once more, to draw back the corner of the drapes and peer outside, searching for anyone who may be watching outside. I see no gunmen, no suspicious cars, no shadowy figures under a streetlight.

As silently as I came, I leave, pulling the window back down into place and picking up the crowbar.

Megan is safe. *For now.*

MEGAN

THERE'S a knock at my door. I don't get up straight away as I don't want to seem too keen, but truth be told, I've been sitting here in my emerald green tea-dress with the white Peter Pan collar and matching white heels for at least an hour.

It was the first time since coming to Galena that I've bought clothes. I've been living in the same cycle of five outfits I brought with me from Maryland ever since I got here—just the basics.

Shopping for the perfect dress was a challenge. *What would Tammy Miller wear?* At first, I'd been looking for something my sweet and wholesome alter ego would buy, but then my train of thought changed. *I am Tammy Miller.* What do I want to wear now that I get to start again? How do I want to look? What do I want people to think of me?

When I was young, I relished the feel of wet-look leggings and sky-high heels, mini-skirts and crop tops, fitted leather jackets and skinny jeans. I was young, hot, and I wanted everybody to see my perfect body in its prime. Even as a fifteen and sixteen-year-old, I reveled in my own sexuality;

built a life around my ability to bring men to their knees, until the wrong man brought me to mine.

Now, I want more substance. I've still got it; I believe that. My legs are long and shapely, my stomach is flat, my small chest is perky. Since leaving Calvin, my skin looks refreshed and healthier, my eyes are starting to shine again, and I like my new hair. If I wanted to dress in something with a plummeting neckline and three-inch heels, I know I'd still drop jaws.

But...I've envisioned the life I yearn for over many years. It's an ordinary, wholesome, family life like the one I might have had if I'd listened to my father's advice and given in to my mother's pleas and gone to college and met a decent man.

In my fantasy, I'm a nurturing wife and mother, a wonderful cook; the kind of woman who can keep plants alive and make them flourish, the sort of woman who is an angel on the streets and a devil in the sheets. All that rebellion in me will be targeted into creativity, travel, and making love in phenomenal ways to one good man.

On the surface, though, I—Tammy Miller—will be a sweet girl. There is no cleavage on show in my little tea dress; my make-up is light with only a modest dash of purple lipstick and a slight flick of mascara. The heels I've chosen are a reasonable height, but enough to show off those long, shapely legs all the same. I feel beautiful.

After a count of three, I stand up and go to the door. When I open it, I'm pleased to see Mark is also dressed up in smart gray pants and a white button-up shirt. He's clean-shaven, his hair combed and styled. He's holding a bottle of red wine and a gorgeous bouquet of flowers.

"For my gracious host."

I take them from him and feel dizzy with glee from the sight and scent of the beautiful blue, lilac and white chrysanthemums, freesia and three large and delicate white roses.

"Mark, that's so sweet of you. Thank you. Come in!"

I step back to let Mark in. He pauses in the doorway and leans forward to kiss my cheek. "You look beautiful."

"I didn't know whether to dress up for a dinner at my place. I thought I'd make the effort."

"Just for me?"

His tone is cheeky and playful. It makes me laugh as I take the flowers through to the kitchen to prepare them for a vase. He comes to stand in the kitchen doorway and watch me. I can see his glance traveling up my legs, and I bite down on my smile. *I want him to look.*

"I'm glad I did, seeing as you bought flowers just for me."

"Honestly, I don't know what I'd have done if I hadn't run into you. I've been floating in a void since I got here; not knowing anyone and having nowhere to begin."

"You and me both." I turn over my shoulder to offer him a reassuring smile. "It's been nice to have some company. I'm glad you came."

"Can I help you with dinner?"

"Flowers, wine and an offer to help? You are a wonderful gentleman, Mark."

"Just making up for my misspent youth."

I laugh. I highly doubt Mark has had so much as a misspent hour in his life. "You can slice the mushrooms if you like."

"What are we having?"

"Mushroom pasta."

"That sounds divine."

"It used to be my go-to date-night dish."

Mark smiles, a mischievous gleam in his eye. "I didn't realize this was a date."

"Oh really?" I hold one of the freshly cut roses to my nose and breathe in softly, keeping my gaze on Mark. "I guess I just read into such lovely flowers."

He takes a step closer. "Okay, I kind of knew it was a date."

Standing on my tiptoes, I plant a kiss on his lips. "Of course it's a date. Date three, by my count."

I turn back to the flowers and continue cutting down the stalks. My heart is racing with anticipation and delight. I've never felt freer or more like myself. Here I am, in a gorgeous ivy dress, cooking dinner in a beautiful, clean apartment, flirting like a normal human being with cute jokes and sideways glances. *This is how life should be.*

We continue to chat and flirt while we cook dinner together. Once we're finished, I pull out one side of the drop-leaf table against the wall of my living room and light a candle then pour two glasses of wine.

"Wow," Mark says, letting out an impressed whistle. "This is a five-star establishment."

"I wanted to give you a break from that motel vibe."

"I'm being truly spoiled."

"Sit. Eat. Enjoy."

Mark pulls out my chair for me before he takes his own seat. My heart flutters again at being treated with such respect. I feel like a real lady; like this pretty dress isn't just a disguise but the perfect fit for the new me.

"So, tell me, Mark, when you were a kid, what did you want to be when you grew up?"

"Straight in there with the big questions. Wow."

I chuckle. "I'm serious! You know, when life throws big changes at you, it's worth going back to figure out who you used to want to be."

"I wanted to be an artist."

"Really?"

"Oh yeah. I even won a scholarship to art school once."

Be still my beating heart. A gentleman and an artist. "What happened?"

He takes a swig of wine and shrugs. "Life got in the way. I had other priorities."

"Like what?"

"Family stuff."

"Oh." I fall silent. I don't want to pry.

Mark smiles. "I know. Instant conversation killer, right? Family—who'd have them?"

"You seem to have done alright on your own, anyway."

He raises a glass. "To making it on your own."

We drink. I'm feeling close to Mark right now. In this moment, I feel a real connection building. Here we are, two strangers on the start of a new journey; beginning alone, but somehow crossing paths. *This is what love feels like.*

I start to feel flushed as the wine goes to my head. Mark must be feeling the same as he rolls up the sleeves of his shirt. Once again, I see the tattoo sleeves from shoulder to wrist on each arm. Now I've got a chance to really examine them.

They're black and white and beautifully done. One arm shows the four horsemen of the apocalypse marching out of storm clouds. The other arm depicts soldiers on the front line. They're dark, terrifying, and somber images and the last thing I expected to see on the skin of this sweet, kind man.

Mark catches me looking and follows my gaze. "More evidence of my misspent youth."

I reach out and trace a finger across the art. "They're incredible."

"I noticed yours the other night."

I laugh, pull out my chair and inch up my skirt. On my thigh is a piece about the size of my hand; a colorful Alice in Wonderland portrait.

"Alice in Wonderland." Mark smiles. "Is there a story behind that?"

"It was my favorite book as a child. I loved the chaos. It was like one big drug trip."

"A drug trip? I thought you were a nice girl."

I touch his tattoo again. "I didn't expect you to have horsemen on your arm. What's the story behind that?"

"I don't really know." He runs his own palm across his forearm. "Something about death and destiny and destruction."

The words stick in my mouth. There is clearly more to Mark than first meets the eye. I'm starting to doubt his stories of leaving his old life due to a break-up. I know how to spot a troubled man.

Yet...I don't care. No man could be worse than Calvin. And few men would have seen and done half the things I've seen and done. The only reason I'm in Illinois instead of behind bars myself is because of the immunity deal I made in exchange for turning against Calvin.

Mark is here for a fresh start, and so am I. I don't care what came before. I won't ask questions of him, and I'll hold my breath, hoping he doesn't ask too many questions of me.

All I want is to feel some joy and closeness in these tattered remnants of a life.

That's why I didn't run. That's why I'm here.

Mark feels like my last hope at happiness, and every risk is worth the chance of being happy at last.

JACK

"Would you design me a tattoo sometime?"

"For you?"

"Yeah, why not?" Megan looks up at me with adoring eyes.

Dinner is done and the plates are clear, pushed to one side so we can rest our elbows on the table. We've been talking for the last hour, but it feels like minutes. I should be on the edge of my seat, knowing assassins are most likely on their way, but the wine and easy company make me feel more relaxed than I can ever remember being.

My home life growing up wasn't easy and relaxed. Nor were the fourteen years I spent behind bars. My vicious, violent stepfather wasn't good company, and Sparky, the other inmates, and the prison guards were hardly great company either.

Megan is a pleasant relief from a hard-lived life. If I came here with half a will to protect her, now it has become a vow. No matter who she walked alongside in her past, no matter what she's done, she doesn't deserve to die.

And I've fallen for her. Hard.

"And what kind of tattoo would you want, Tammy?"

"I don't know. Something about regeneration. Regrowth. Redemption."

"Those are some pretty big themes."

"Maybe a phoenix or something."

"Or maybe Alice, when she returns from behind the looking glass."

Megan's face lights up. "That's intuitive. I love the sound of that."

"In my experience, no matter how much people change, a part of them is always just who they were."

"That's a depressing thought."

"I don't think so. We were all born pure."

She looks at me like I'm a prophet speaking the truest words she's ever heard. I'm only speaking from experience. I used to have good, honest dreams. I used to be a good honest man. If I ever achieve redemption or my own chance to regenerate, that's who I'll be again—just a boy who loves to sketch in his notebook, watching the world go by.

"Tell me more about you," I say. "Before Illinois."

"Well, I grew up in Eureka Springs in Arkansas."

False.

"My parents ran a little grocery store."

A lie.

"I'm an only child."

Who the hell knows if that's true or not?

"And what else? I want to know about who you were. What your dreams were. What you like and dislike. Not the facts of your life, but who you really are."

"I'm not the only one asking deep questions tonight."

"Is it that deep? I feel like I've just scratched the surface of getting to know you. I want to know it all."

"Fair enough." Megan leans forward on her elbows. Her face looks small and cute in the candlelight. Her eyes catch the glow of the flickering flame. She pushes her hair back behind her ear as she thinks. She has two piercings—one in the lobe and a ring in the cartilage. "I wanted to be—and don't laugh at me—a stunt double."

I do laugh. Then, when I look up and see Megan pouting, I laugh again. "You? A stunt double? Who did you train under? Jackie Chan or Bruce Lee?"

"Shut up! You said you wouldn't laugh." She chucks her napkin at me. "I thought it would be cool." She shrugs. "Motorbikes, jumping off ledges, leaping out of burning buildings...I was always a bit of an adrenaline junkie."

"And how far did you get with that dream?"

She smiles. "Not very."

"There's still time."

"I think my chances to kick ass and cheat death on film have passed me by. I found other ways to get my adrenaline fixes instead."

"Oh yeah?" *Maybe she'll finally let slip something about her ex-lover, and I can figure out how a nice girl like this ended up mixing with trash like him.*

"It was another life." She picks up her discarded napkin and places it back on her plate. "I grew up and moved on."

"So what are you into now? What do you enjoy?"

"Horror movies and cheese."

"A classic combination."

She laughs. I love the sound of it, so genuine and easy.

"Not necessarily together, but a cheeseboard and a bit of del Toro sounds amazing."

"Sounds like an idea for our next date."

She bites down on her smile—a little habit of hers I've noticed in our short time together.

"I like that you're already planning the next date. I thought maybe I went in a bit strong on our last one."

"No stronger than me, and I think this one is going well, too. Don't you?"

"Absolutely." She stands, the two finished plates in her hands. "Should we watch a movie?"

"Only if it's a horror with cheese."

"I can offer a thriller with chips."

"Deal."

Five minutes later, we're sitting side by side on Megan's sofa, watching some film with De Niro in it. I'm not really interested in the movie. All I can think about is Megan's body close to mine. I put my arm around her and pull her closer.

She smiles, kicks off her heels and pulls her feet up underneath her, leaning into my chest.

Something in me thaws. I never had time for real relationships before I ended up in prison. To feel the softness of a woman pressed against me inspires something that feels almost like hope.

Snap out of it, Jack. You'll be back behind bars before you know it, and the next time you're holding Megan, it could be her corpse. Don't get attached.

MEGAN

MARK'S warm body feels so good against my skin. I rest my cheek on his chest and feel like I could fall straight into the deepest and most wonderful sleep. I feel completely safe and completely at home with him.

Calvin had no emotion. He didn't know empathy, compassion, fear, or love. Mark seems to be full of genuine emotion. His troubled soul speaks to mine, and I want to stay with him where I feel at peace.

"There's something about you, Mark," I whisper. "It's like I knew you in another life."

He tightens his arms around me. "I know what you mean. I feel like I know you already."

I twist to look into his eyes. He's gazing at me through the dim light, longing in his eyes. I'm filled with longing too —to be close to someone and to feel some pleasure. Sex with Calvin stopped being pleasurable the second I realized what a monster I was and the second the love between us disappeared. I was nothing but a toy to him; sex was a show of obedience, not of love.

Not tonight.

Tonight, I'm going to wrap my arms around a man who's been kind to me and sink into new levels of bliss because I'm free and because I can.

I kiss him.

Mark doesn't hesitate to kiss me back. He places his hand on the back of my head and pulls me closer toward him, moving his lips over mine and pressing down with intense passion. In the background, the movie comes to an end and the credits roll, casting a new darkness across the room.

I push his lips open and press my tongue into his mouth. He still tastes of wine; his breath is warm. I run my fingers desperately through his hair. Every time I touch him, I feel a rush of blood downwards. My panties are growing wet.

Mark places his hands on my waist, his fingers gripping tightly. I enjoy the sensation of being held so tightly, of being so desired. I straddle him. I can already feel the hardness of him through his pants rubbing against me between my legs. My breath comes faster. I've never been so turned on.

He reaches under my skirt and pulls down my panties. I let them slide down my legs then kick them off. I'm still straddling Mark as he slides his palm up my inner thigh, then runs a finger along my skin, pushing inward and seeking a certain spot.

He finds it. He presses his finger down against my clit. He moans when he feels how wet I am. The movement of his finger rubbing against me feels silky and warm. I arch my back and let my head fall back, sighing in pleasure while Mark strokes my clit.

"You like that?"

"Mmm."

"God, you're so wet."

I bow my head down to kiss him, letting my hair brush against his face. He lets out a low moan of pleasure; I can hear the hunger in the sound.

Suddenly, he pushes me off of him to the other side of the couch and kneels on the floor. Knowing what's coming, I eagerly spread my legs and lean back against the cushions, hitching up my skirt to expose myself to him.

Marks places his hands on my inner knees and pushes my legs further apart. He presses his finger against my clit, then moves down to push two fingers inside me. He moves them in and out while keeping his gaze fixed on mine. I shudder when he pulls his fingers out and sucks them clean before leaning his head down between my legs and running his tongue against my clit.

He finds it straight away, and before he starts to lick, he sucks, making my clit swell and throb until I'm gasping with eager anticipation. He flicks his tongue against my swollen bud then presses down harder, licking and stroking until I moan.

As I moan, he groans too, reacting to every sound of pleasure I release with sounds of his own. We're a symphony of lust and desire.

He licks in steady, rhythmic strokes.

"Harder." I press my hand down on the back of his head to bring his tongue and mouth closer to my body.

Mark holds onto my legs and eagerly pleases me with more fervor.

I start to whimper in pleasure. "Don't stop! Jesus, don't stop."

The orgasm comes only moments later, crashing over my body until I'm shuddering. He doesn't stop then but rubs at my clit with his thumb until the feeling builds again. I'm squirming and gasping, trying to close my legs, but not wanting him to stop, glad when he continues to rub until the wave crashes again, leaving me limp and on fire.

Mark stands up. With shaking hands, I reach for his belt, unbuckling it and pulling apart the two leather strips. I pull down his pants and briefs together, releasing his swollen, pulsing cock.

I whimper with desire at the sight of it. Mark kicks off his briefs, pants, shoes, and socks, then pulls his shirt off over his head. As he steps toward me, I reach out and take his cock in my hand. He moans at my touch. I pull him toward me and lick his tip, then up and down the smooth skin of his shaft. When I take him into my warm mouth, he gasps. He's huge and hard, the anticipation of what is to come making me even wetter.

My eyes glance up to see him watching me. I smirk.

He strokes my hair. "You are so fucking hot baby doll."

There's another tattoo on the right of his chest—a glorious ship with sails high in the wind and crashing waves beneath it. I press my palm against the ink, feeling my own waves still crashing inside. I can't wait any longer. My mouth releases his cock so I can speak.

"There's a condom in the bathroom drawer." *From the pack I bought after we first had sex.*

Mark dashes to the bathroom and returns, condom in hand. I laugh at the look of eagerness on his face. *Me too, baby.*

He pushes me back against the sofa cushions once more, holding his cock in one hand and guiding it inside me. He enters in one swift, deep thrust that fills me entirely. I cry out in pleasure and surprise at how big he feels as I take all of him in at once.

Mark throws one of my legs over his shoulder and pounds into me. I'm still tingling from the two orgasms, and the feeling of his dick inside me makes me lightheaded. I grip onto his shoulder and grind my hips into him, wanting him deeper still.

"Fuck me, Tammy," Mark moans. "You're going to make me cum."

He pulls out, grabs me by the hips and flips me over so

I'm kneeling on the seat of the sofa. He reaches for the zipper of my dress and pulls it down, then pulls the sleeves from my shoulders and the dress away from my body. I step out of it then resume my position kneeling on the sofa, my elbows on the back cushions.

With one hand on my back, Mark pushes me forward, bending me over. I spread my legs, widening my stance. He enters me again, so deeply and so fast I have to grip onto the cushions to steady myself. I don't hold back my cries of pleasure.

Mark traces his hand across my bare ass, teasing me with a gentle slap. I press back against him, desperate for his cock. *I can't remember the last time anything felt this good.*

"Fuck me, Mark. Please," I whisper. I cup my breasts that hang down, and I caress them as he toys with me. I moan as the sensation from my nipples waves through me.

I let him fuck me until he starts to breathe faster and shudder. I know he's going to cum. Before he can, I pull away and turn around.

"I want to ride you."

His eyes are wide with wonder, and he eagerly lies on his back on the sofa. I straddle him and sink down onto his cock, easing myself down slowly, letting him fill me inch by inch. From here, I have the perfect view of his toned, lean body. I drink in the sight of his rippling biceps, the soft shadow of a six pack on his abdomen, the raw desire in his eyes.

I watch him bite down on his lip and moan. His gaze travels over my breasts, down to my pussy and back up again. He grips onto my thighs as I gyrate against him. He's already so close to cumming, I purposefully slow down, taking my sweet time to draw an orgasm from him.

Mark grabs my hips and tries to make me rock faster.

"I'm so close."

I lean down and whisper playfully in his ear. "I know."

He laughs, then groans. "You're a tease, Tammy Miller."

"You love it."

"Mmm... You know I do."

I tease him until I'm the one who can't take it any longer and I begin to grind fast, hard and deep, until Mark throws his head back, cries out and grips onto my hips. I stay with him deep inside me as he shudders in the aftermath.

Finally, I step off him and fall naked against him on the sofa. He pulls me against him, brushing back my hair and kissing my forehead, which is damp with sweat.

"Nobody's ever going to hurt you while I'm around."

I don't look up, but bury my head in his chest. Is that something normal men say after sex; the type of men who don't abuse and take advantage of trusting women? Or is it something more?

My past has made me paranoid. I can't bear to lose the first good thing that's happened to me since I was a girl because I'm too broken to believe someone can be genuinely good.

I just want to stay here with him.

JACK

I WAKE up to the smell of bacon. The salty scent makes me salivate, and I lick my lips as I sit up and rub my eyes. I'm tangled in Megan's bedsheets, but she's nowhere to be seen.

"Tammy?"

Megan appears around the doorway. "Good morning, sleepy head."

"What time is it?"

"Almost midday."

"You're kidding?"

She laughs. "What have either of us got to do today? You must have needed to sleep in. Breakfast will be ready in five."

"It smells amazing."

Megan's wearing nothing but an oversized T-shirt as a nightdress. I trail my gaze up her long shapely legs and her toned body, picturing the bare skin underneath it, remembering last night. My eyes travel to her face. I see she's smiling, enjoying being admired. Her hair is tousled and her eyes shadowy from the smudged remnants of last night's eyeliner. She's got an all-natural, just-out-of-bed look and it's sexy as hell. I've only just woken up, but I'm hard again.

"You should have woken me up."

"Why? You were out cold."

I feel guilty for having slept in when I'm here to protect Megan. I can't protect her from anything when I'm passed out in her bed. I step out of bed, pull on my jeans and follow her into the small kitchen.

She's standing at the stove, a large pan filled with thick, glazed slabs of bacon spitting oil and another is waiting for fresh eggs. Gazing around the kitchen, I also see a carton of orange juice, freshly-baked uncut bread, Greek yogurt, and fruit.

"Have you been out this morning?"

"I thought I'd feed you."

I go to her, place my hands on her shoulders and kiss her forehead. "My mouth's watering."

"It's almost ready." She picks up an egg and cracks it in two with a fork, letting the egg spill into the second pan and start to sizzle.

I could kick myself for sleeping the whole morning while Megan's been out on her own. Anything could have happened. She could have been killed. I need to be more vigilant.

I couldn't stand to lose her. I've never felt close to a woman before; I've never felt close to anyone. Megan is the first person to make me feel like a human, capable of loving and being loved. That one day that was everything is quickly turning into a person who is everything.

While the breakfast finishes cooking, Megan slides a couple of newspapers across the counter to me. "I've already had a thumb through the want ads. The apartments, too. Looks like there are a few nice places popping up."

I accept the paper and flick through the first few pages. "Sure, but I won't know what my budget is until I find work."

It's all bullshit. Every word I'm saying is complete crap,

yet it's spilling out naturally. I could so easily be someone else; someone without a conviction, without a torrid history; just some ordinary guy who's met a girl and has nothing to worry about except deciding how long to wait before calling her after going back to his motel.

"I was actually going to suggest an activity for today." She leans her elbows on the counter and looks up at me with her smudged puppy dog eyes and a hopeful smile. "I thought we could go job-hunting together. I was thinking we could take a nice stroll through Galena, hand out some resumés... I've got a printer here—you could print some copies off."

"I haven't got anything saved. I'll come for the walk though. Maybe I'll see some 'Help Wanted' signs while we're out."

My cell, still in my pocket from last night, buzzes. I pull it out and look at the screen. I have three missed calls from William. I was due for my parole meeting an hour ago. I swallow and slide my cell back into my pocket. My blood is running cold. The moment of weakness I had when I allowed Sparky to convince me becoming an assassin was something I was remotely capable of will ruin my whole life a second time.

At least there might still be time to save Megan's.

We eat breakfast together. Since leaving prison, every meal tastes amazing, but Megan is one hell of a cook. I would gladly let her cook for me forever—or at least until my time on the run comes to an end. William will go looking for me at Sparky's when I'm a no-show—that's the address I gave when I had to register where I'd be living when I was released.

"Last night was something, wasn't it?" Megan says as we eat side by side at the drop-leaf table where we shared a romantic meal together the night before. She looks across the table at me with wide doe eyes. I can see the contentment shining in them.

"It really was."

"I hope your journey of self-reinvention keeps you in Galena."

"I can't believe you want to keep seeing me."

She sits up straighter, her fork poised above her plate. "Why on earth would you say something like that after the time we've spent together? I don't think I've been too subtle in making it clear I'm into you, Mark. Like, in a pretty big way."

"I'm into you, too. In a major way." I kiss her forehead." "I just didn't think I was that much of a catch—unemployed, nowhere to live. I wasn't expecting anyone to be interested for a long time."

It's not too far from the truth. I'm an unemployed, homeless convict with a past that's about to catch up with him once again. If Megan knew the real me, she'd run a mile. Still, I enjoy the fantasy. This is what my life could have been like if my mother had fallen for a man instead of a monster.

And why the hell are you still here, Megan? What is keeping you in Galena? It can't be me, can it? Don't stay for me. You're risking your life.

"You're starting over. There's no shame in that." Megan shrugs and flicks a bacon rind at me to lighten the mood. I laugh and flick some orange juice off my finger at her. The solemn moment passes.

We eat breakfast together, continuing to flirt and joke around. It's easy and comfortable—I almost forget I'm here for a reason.

When breakfast is done, we share a steamy shower, get dressed and head out.

"What kind of work are you looking for?" I ask Megan.

"Anything. I just want to get out of the house."

We start heading down toward North Main Street—a fair way away from Megan's home, but I'm not against a walk in the fresh air.

She's right—Galena is a beautiful city. There is greenery everywhere, wide spacious streets, clean sidewalks. Even the skies are blue. But most beautiful of all is Megan. She's wearing a cute teal sundress with a pair of gray ankle boots and a white slightly oversized cardigan. She looks excited and joyful. No matter what Sparky or that dossier may have told me about her, I know this woman is nothing but good. She's a ray of sunshine in this world.

Instinctively, I hold out my hand to her. She slips her fingers around mine and squeezes. I smile. It's a small gesture of acceptance, but more than I ever remember being shared with me. I'm not going to leave her for a second. She will not be torn from my arms. I'm going to protect her with every breath in my body.

I take a deep breath of the fresh Illinois air and let my shoulders relax, but my calm is short-lived. Lifting my gaze, I spot a man across the street who doesn't look like he belongs on this quiet residential street. He has a poorly kept beard, a dirty bomber jacket and oversized jeans that are shredded at the bottom from being caught under heel.

Did I once see him doing meth in Sparky's house?

It's not his appearance that puts me on edge, but the intensity in the way he's staring at us; more specifically, the way his gaze is lingering on Megan with a cold, brutal focus. He reaches inside his jacket.

"Get down!"

I throw myself over Megan and barrel her to the ground. She screams and starts to push me off her.

"What the hell?"

Her anger is short-lived. She hears the bullet fire and sees the window shatter the second she's on the ground. Her eyes are wide and terrified. She looks for the shooter.

I don't stop to investigate. I scramble to my feet and pull

her up roughly by her wrist. I don't have time to be gentle. This is life or death.

"Come with me."

I drag her after me down one block after another. If the streets hadn't been as quiet as they were that weekday morning, I have no doubt I'd have been attacked and pulled away from her. I look like a kidnapper, pulling a sobbing woman roughly after me down the street with relentless determination while she cries her eyes out.

I must have pulled her after me for twenty minutes before I feel like I can pause. I drag her with me into an isolated side street and grip her fiercely, catching her eye with a wild stare.

"Pull yourself together, Megan. Someone is trying to kill you."

She gasps when she hears her own, real name coming from my lips. Her resistance fails, and she goes limp in my arms.

"Who are you?"

MEGAN

I PULL MYSELF TOGETHER. My wrist is aching from how tightly Mark had grabbed me. I can already see the red marks turning into bruises. My face is flushed and wet with tears. I drag my palms across my cheeks and wipe my face dry, sniffing and swallowing until the lump in my throat disappears, although my heart doesn't stop racing.

We're in some alley where no eyes are watching; where anything can happen—and I have no idea whether I trust this man.

If he knows who I am—who I *really* am—then he can only be on one of two sides: sent by witness protection or sent by Calvin.

I tuck my hair behind my ear, straighten up and clear my throat. Mark's seen me panic, but now I want to stand tall and let him see me defiant and unafraid. If he has been sent by Calvin, then I won't give him the satisfaction of seeing me cower and cry.

"Meeting me wasn't a mistake, was it? You've been following me."

"Yes."

Mark's face is stone. There is no expression, no clue in his features to tell me whether he's a friend or an enemy. I think of the conversations we had in the café, the romantic dinner we shared at my condo, last night when we fucked... Who is this man?

He lets go of me and goes to the head of the alley to peer out onto the main street, scanning for danger. I consider running, but I don't know if I'm safer with or without him. If Mark wanted to kill me, why would he have saved me from that bullet?

My mouth is dry, and my head is swimming. *Someone tried to kill me*. Not someone—Calvin. Whether he was the gunman or not, it doesn't take a genius to figure out that the only person who'd want me dead is my vicious, criminal ex. He'd do anything to save himself; even kill me.

"I need to know who you are."

Mark returns to the alley, pacing up and down like a caged animal. I can see the dilemma playing out behind his eyes and the tension in the way he clasps and unclasps his fists and lets out a low growl of frustration.

"You don't need to know."

"Forget whoever just tried to kill me. I slept with you last night—and I don't even know who the fuck you are."

"I'll tell you everything when we're somewhere safe. For now, all you need to know is that I'm here to protect you."

"Are you a US Marshall?"

"No."

"Then who sent you?"

"It doesn't matter. I'm a friend."

"Of course, it matters. You want me to trust you after what just happened? You called me Megan—and nobody's supposed to know who I am."

"Megan Cartwright. You used to date a dangerous man."

My breath comes in shudders. I'm terrified, and I don't

know what I should do. I stare at Mark's handsome face; the kindness and affection in it have been replaced with an intensity and darkness I've not seen before. He rolls his sleeves up to focus on the job at hand, and I see those ominous tattoos on his skin once more. He looks like the hero from an action movie, his jaw set in determination, his hair pushed back, his body poised to fight... but is he the hero of this chaos?

"And what's your real name?"

He grunts. "Jack."

"Why did you lie to me?"

"It was for your own protection. Enough questions. We need to keep moving. Come with me."

"How do I know I'm safe?"

"I've spent the last few days trailing you everywhere you've gone to make sure you don't end up with a bullet in your head. I've watched you day and night. I've made sure nobody touches you. Last night I was in your bed. If I wanted you dead, I'd have slit your throat in your sleep."

His words make my blood run cold. They're intended to make me feel safer, but all they do is make me realize this man isn't afraid to kill.

"I don't know you."

"You don't need to. There's a man out there with a gun who's searching for you right now. All I care about is getting you as far away from him as possible."

As much as I fear him, I believe him. If Mark—*Jack*— wanted me dead, he'd had plenty of opportunities. And if it wasn't for him, I'd already have been killed by the man who tried to shoot me.

Right now, Jack's the best hope I have for survival, and I've not come this far to give up now. I'm going to make sure Calvin pays for what he's done, but to do that, I need to stay alive.

"Fine. Let's get out of here." I stride past him to the head of the alley and look around. All clear. "But as soon as we're somewhere we can talk, I expect to know everything."

Jack nods and reaches for my hand. I stare at it—the same hand that pulled me into the most intense kiss of my life last night and stroked my hair in the night. I know now it's the hand of a complete stranger.

I take it.

We run, flying down the streets faster than I've ever run.

"Where are we going?" I gasp. There's a stitch in my side I'm clutching, doubled over. Jack tugs me along after him, and I have to straighten up and run once more.

"The bus station. There's one on Bartell Boulevard."

"The bus station?"

"You can't stay in Galena."

We reach the bus station within the hour, and Jack asks for my cell.

"Why?"

"I need to order tickets."

"Where are we going?"

"Chicago."

"What's in Chicago?"

"It's the end of the line. I want to put as much distance between you and whoever was sent to kill you as possible."

He takes my cell from me and takes out the sim card, replacing it with his own,

"It's not bugged, but best to be safe."

"Why use my cell at all?"

Jack pulls out his own brick of a cell. "Mine's a cheap burner without internet access."

"How do you know my cell isn't bugged?"

"I swept your condo for bugs. It's clear."

"When did you sweep my condo? Before we had sex? After? When I was cooking breakfast?"

Jack frowns. "Does it matter?" He takes my hand and

pulls me toward the gas station near the bus stop. "Act natural."

I try to keep calm as Jack takes my hands and grips it tightly, making me stand by the edge of the gas station in an uncomfortable wait.

"If anyone gives you so much as a funny look, you run." Jack glances up and down the station where all the Greyhound buses are lined up, ready to depart or just pulling in. "Whoever it is might guess we're making a run for it. Hopefully, he'll assume we're in a car."

I'm starting to get cold in my summer dress and cardigan. A chilly wind has picked up. I pull the material more tightly around my body, staying silent. Glancing across at me, Jack sees I'm cold and puts his arm around me. The smell of his cologne takes me back to last night, but the memory isn't a sweet one anymore. I push his arm off me and step away to put distance between us.

"You should stay close to me." Jack glances at his watch. "We have fifteen minutes. You want anything to drink or eat? It's a four-hour trip."

"I'm fine."

"You're right. Best not to risk missing it."

I examine his face. He looks tired and defeated; on edge. He's restless; can't stay still. He keeps scanning the same areas over and over again—the gas station, the Walmart parking lot, the boulevard.

"That bullet was so close I've got glass in my hair," he mutters. "Shit. I really thought you were safe for the time being. I didn't even see that guy out there. I should have spotted him before we stepped outside, but I got complacent. I didn't even check before we opened the door."

I clench my jaw and fold my arms across my chest. "It's about time you tell me who you are."

"Not yet."

"Once I'm on that bus, I'm stuck with you until Chicago."

"I'm not going to hurt you. Especially not in front of a bus full of people. Want to pat me down? I'm not armed."

"A guy like you could strangle me to death. You don't need a weapon."

He looks wounded. His air of drama and intensity drops, and he looks at me with defeated eyes. "Do you really think I'd ever hurt you?"

"I don't know the first thing about you."

"That's probably for the best."

"I need to know who you are."

"Soon."

JACK

I DON'T BLAME Megan for being scared. Anyone would be in her situation. I've outed myself as a liar, and she's got every reason to be distrusting.

The bus arrives. I make her wait until everyone else has boarded so I can examine each person who boards before we get on.

"Nobody looks suspicious."

"How would you know?" Megan scoffs. "I thought you were an ordinary guy."

She pushes past me and steps up onto the bus. Her words are sharp, but I deserve it. I let her walk down the aisle and choose where she wants to sit. She takes a window seat and I sit beside her, looking up and down the bus one more time.

The bus is in good condition with pleasant air conditioning. The leather seats are clean. I feel dirty in yesterday's clothes and worry that I look a mess. I'm sweating from having run so far, and I can feel the damp patches under my arms and on my back. I must look conspicuous.

Megan must feel the same. As soon she sits down, she takes out a compact mirror from her purse and readjusts her hair and makeup. She does so in silence, finally clipping the mirror shut again and putting it away without a word.

Neither of us says a thing until the bus starts moving.

"There goes the place that was meant to be home," Megan says bitterly. "I guess I should have known better than to think I could disappear into a happy ever after that easily."

"I promise you're going to be safe."

"Funny enough, I don't think your promises count for much."

"I'm not here to hurt you."

"I've got no idea why you're here. If you were witness protection, you'd have identified yourself by now. Which means you're someone else. But I don't know who." She blinks back tears. "I should have left when I got that note."

It's time to come clean. I turn to Megan and lower my voice. "My name is Jack Woodson, and I was hired to kill you."

Her eyes grow wide, her breathing comes fast. She stands. "Excuse me."

I grab her by the wrist and pull her back down into her seat. I hate being the one to set off that terror in her eyes, but I can't let her cause a scene and risk drawing attention to herself.

"Listen to me," I say in a low, steady voice. "I don't know who it was who asked me to kill you. All I know is that I was sent. As soon as I made it to Galena and met you, I knew I couldn't do it. You don't deserve to die at the hands of someone like me. I returned to Baltimore and told the middleman who set up the *arrangement* that there was no deal."

Megan swallows, her eyes glazed with tears. "And what would have been the reward for killing me?"

"A hundred and fifty thousand dollars."

She falls silent. I can see her trying to process what she's hearing. She blinks back tears and stares out the window in silence for a long while. We've got four hours to kill so I give her time to absorb the life-shattering news.

"And you were going to do it?"

I squeeze the top of my nose between my fingers and close my eyes. "I don't know. I didn't want to, but things were hopeless." I lick my dry lips. "I've just got out of prison. I have nobody; nothing. The money sounded good."

"It sounded like you had a good deal on the table—the life of a stranger to turn your own life around." Her gaze is defiant now. "Why didn't you do it?"

I tear my gaze away. "I'm not a killer. And...Fuck, Megan. You've got under my skin. I care about you. None of that was a lie. That day...it really was everything."

"So you decided not to kill me. I don't understand why you're still here."

"I just told you: I care. Besides, someone else will take my place. I've not met this ex of yours, but I'm sure you know that much is true."

She nods. "Calvin is merciless."

"Calvin? Is that his name?"

"Calvin Raynor."

I draw is a sharp breath through my teeth. Calvin Raynor is the man who tried to hire me. I've never met him, but his name was commonplace around the joint. Half the people in there had worked for him or walked in circles with those who did. I'd heard stories about the guy—a ruthless mob boss who'd kill anyone to get to the top and secure his place as the toughest bastard in Maryland.

"You used to date Calvin Raynor?"

"I think 'date' is the wrong way to put it." Megan looks down at her knees and smooths down her skirt obsessively. She sniffs back further tears. "I was his."

"I came back to protect you."

"Why?"

I shake my head and lift my hands in a hopeless shrug. "I don't know. Call it redemption. After everything I've been through in my life, I've held onto the belief that I'm not an evil man. The day I agreed to hunt you down—like an animal —I had a glimpse of how evil I could be. I can't live with that. Knowing I'm a good person, deep down, is all that got me through the fourteen years behind bars. I knew I could hold my head high because I wasn't really like the rapists and murderers inside. I was a victim of circumstance." I swallow, feeling a lump rise in my throat. "Prison changed me. It unlocked a darkness. I came out bitter. I needed to get back to the man I was before I was put away."

"So all this is about you, then?" Megan rolls her eyes. "I should have guessed."

"You're wrong." I turn back to her and meet her eyes with fire in my own. I drink in her flushed, defiant expression; the beauty in her pale eyes. I feel the warmth in the memory of her touch. "It didn't take long for you to mean something to me. You're a good person in a bad world, Megan. We have to protect what little goodness there is in this fucked up world. I wasn't going to walk away just to let someone else put your light out."

"How noble."

"I'm not fucking with you." I drum my fingers on my knee. "I care about you."

"You came to Illinois to kill me."

"And I came back to save you."

"You think that makes it okay?"

I shake my head. "I read a dossier on you before I was sent to Galena." I look across at her for her reaction. She's listening intently, the landscape of Illinois rolling by behind her. "It said you were with Calvin for more than ten years."

"So?"

"You're obviously not opposed to keeping company with guilty men."

"It's different."

"Is it? Is watching someone torture and kill any different from pulling the trigger yourself?" I slouch down in my seat to get comfy. "At least I walked away and refused."

Megan's eyes fill with tears and her chin trembles as they fall. "That's not fair."

"Isn't it? What was it that made you decide to testify? Were you just trying to save your own skin? Had things got too hot in the kitchen? Why didn't you do it years before?"

"No matter what I have or haven't done, it doesn't change the fact you came to my home to kill me."

"No, it doesn't."

I feel guilty for making her cry; I've clearly touched a nerve. It makes me question just what Megan has done in her life. Has she hurt people? Has she let people get hurt? I can see the shame in the way the tears keep flowing, no matter how much she dabs at her eyes with a tissue from her purse.

"You're wrong about me," Megan says at last. She takes a deep breath and looks me square in the eye. "I do deserve to die."

I pause a moment, letting the pain in her voice cut through the layers of hate I've let myself become wrapped up in down to the spark of empathy that still lives inside.

"I'm not going to let that happen."

MEGAN

WE'RE BOTH EMOTIONALLY and physically exhausted by the time we reach Harrison Street in Chicago and disembark from the bus. I'm scared to set my feet on the sidewalk in case another hitman is hiding around a corner or some sniper is perched on a roof. I wait for the bullets to rain down, but none come.

I wait for Jack to get off the bus, too. I'm done trying to run from him. I don't believe he is here to hurt me—not anymore. Clearly, he's a dangerous and guilty man—but I'm not an innocent woman. Jack is right—at least he walked away. Not like me.

"What time will Khosa meet you?"

I sent a message to Khosa while we were traveling to let him know what had happened.

"5 p.m. at the Congress Plaza Hotel. He's booked me a room under the name Amy Blythe." I pause. "I guess this is where you disappear?"

"What do you mean?"

"It doesn't seem like you're on the right side of the law currently."

"I'm not going anywhere. Those idiots from witness protection don't know their asses from their elbows. Look at what happened today. They don't have the first idea how to keep you safe."

"You could get arrested."

"I don't give a fuck. Let them put me back behind bars. There's nothing for me on the outside anyway."

I don't know what to say. I can't read Jack. I don't understand him. He's under no obligation to protect me, but he's here. But I can't feel any gratitude for that; he came to kill me. I don't know if he's a guardian angel or a hitman without a gun. I'm on edge, but I don't want him to leave me, either.

He takes my hand, more gently now. It's a relief to feel a kinder touch. Instead of trying to get him off me, I cling to him. He's all I have to hold onto now.

Jack turns to me and offers me a weary smile. "I'm sorry for how rough I was with you today. I just wanted to get you somewhere safe, and I didn't have time to explain."

I don't forgive him, but I acknowledge him with a nod and walk calmly alongside him toward the roadside so we can hail a cab. We get inside and arrive at the Congress Plaza Hotel soon after.

It's an enormous hotel that stretches almost from one side of the street to the other, dominating the road. Looking at the rows and rows of windows, it feels like there must be a thousand rooms inside. *A thousand places for a killer to hide.*

We enter underneath a red canopy emblazoned with the hotel's name and step into the most fabulous marble foyer with impressive columns and incredible furnishings in white and gold. There are dozens of armchairs and a sofa in front of the check-in desk. The ceilings seem to be a mile high and carved in the most glorious arc designs.

I go to the desk, feeling shy in the face of such immense

grandeur. I expected to be holed up on some back-alley dive motel, not somewhere as decadent as this.

"Miss Amy Blythe to check in, please."

The polished and neat front desk attendant smiles brightly. "Of course." She looks like she knows something.

She completes the check-in without asking for ID, and I gladly take my key.

"You're in room 502. Take the elevator to the fifth floor and follow the corridor on the right."

Jack places his hand gently between my shoulders and guides me toward the elevator.

"We're almost there," he says calmly. "Two more minutes and we'll be behind a closed door and safe."

"I hope so."

He walks at my side with strong, confident steps not letting any kind of nerves show. I feel like everyone must be able to tell I'm a mess. My legs are like jelly. After a long day of drama and travel, I've reached my limit and am ready to collapse. I want to close my eyes and sleep.

A few minutes later, we're at the hotel room and inside. Jack closes and bolts the door behind us.

"We made it."

I look around the hotel room. The room is clean and crisp with white walls and fresh white linens on the king-size bed. The floors are an old-fashioned blue carpet with a red patterned border design. Apart from that, the room is fairly bare—only a couple of bedside tables and lamps. The door to the ensuite bathroom is by the entrance to the room.

I sit down on the edge of the bed, then let my body fall back onto the soft mattress. I close my eyes. "Thank God."

Jack walks around the room for a moment, more vigilant than any of the witness protection agents I've met so far. He pulls the drape aside and looks out the window before shutting the drapes entirely.

I sigh. "We're sitting in the dark now?"

"I don't want anyone looking in."

"There are a million windows. Besides, nobody's looking for me here."

"All I know is that someone knew where you were when you were in Galena. Depending on who it is giving out the information, I can't be sure they don't know where you are right now."

I screw my face up, kick my shoes off and curl into the fetal position on the bedcovers. "Don't, Mark. I can't cope with any more terror today. I need to sleep."

"It's Jack."

I sit up again, resting my back against the headboard and cuddling a pillow to my chest. "Of course, it is." I look around the empty hotel room. The silence is deafening. "We're alone now. Maybe I can hear some more of your story—like how you came to be tasked with killing me."

"You don't need to know any of this, Megan."

"I want to know. I need to understand."

Jack sinks down onto the mattress beside me. I can see the weight of the world on his shoulders. He looks more exhausted than I do. He looks over at me with a weary gaze. "You really want to hear the whole thing?"

"I really do."

"Fine." He lets out a long breath and slaps his hands down on his knees. "It started fourteen years ago when I was charged with killing my stepfather."

I gasp and instinctively draw up my feet closer to my body, the way a child does when they fear there's a monster under the bed about to grab them by the ankles. "I thought you said you weren't a killer?"

"It was self-defense. Kind of."

"Kind of?"

"The bastard was beating my mother to death." Jack runs

both hands through his hair, then puts his head in his hands, resting his elbows on his knees; the very picture of a defeated man. "Beating her harder than ever before, and I'd seen him really give her some. This time, I was certain, he was going to kill her. So I killed him first."

I swallow, trying to clear the huge lump that's formed in my throat. I have a morbid curiosity to know the garish details, but I'm almost too afraid to ask.

"How did you do it?"

"Kill him?" Jack raises an eyebrow and chuckles bitterly. "He was an avid bowler. I picked up his lucky ball and smashed him over the head with it. Split his skull in half like a watermelon." He shakes his head. "That's why they called me Strike in prison."

"That doesn't explain why you were after me."

Jack takes his head out his hands and sits up straighter. "My cellmate was that middleman I told you about."

"The one who arranged the hit with Calvin?"

"Bingo. After I got out, I was really down on my luck. No cash, no family, no place to go. He kept telling me about this 'job' he had for me that was too good to pass up."

"Killing me."

Jack nods.

"No family? What about your mother?"

I see him wince and shake his head in anger. "She killed herself."

"What?"

"Just days after I was convicted."

I bow my head. "I'm sorry."

"Not as sorry as I am. I stayed in that house for years because I couldn't bear to leave her alone with him, too afraid he'd kill her one day. I could have left. I could have made something of myself. Instead, I stayed for her sake, took a fair share of beatings of my own, gave up on all my dreams, and then topped it all off with a manslaughter conviction and fourteen years behind bars for saving her life."

"And she took her own life anyway." My voice is soft and empathetic.

Jack lifts his hands in defeat. "Life's a bitch." He looks across at me and smiles wryly. "You remind me of her."

"Of your mother? How?"

"A woman who got involved with a bad man and now she's in over her head."

I straighten up defiantly and slam the pillow back down into its place on the bed. "I'm not the only one who's in over my head."

"I believe you're a good person, you know," he continues. "Just as naïve as she was."

"Unlike her, you had no obligation to protect me."

"Call it a savior complex. Or I'm just a complete fucking fool."

"Either way, you saved my life today."

JACK

A SMARTER MAN would get out of Dodge now. A US marshal is on his way, and I'm a felon who's broken parole. Not to mention I've corroborated with a dangerous criminal to track down a woman in witness protection with the intent of putting a bullet between her eyes. When that marshal comes, my luck will run out.

Yet I can't leave. For the same reason, I couldn't leave my mother to face her bad choices alone. I can't risk losing Megan. I know that turning my back for just a minute could be a death sentence for her. Look what happened back in Galena—I didn't scan the street and I missed the gunman standing just outside her door.

"I've shown you mine, now you show me yours."

Megan frowns. "What?"

"Your story. How did you get involved with Calvin Raynor?"

"That's easy. I was young and stupid." She moves across the bed to sit beside me, placing her feet on the ground and sitting at my side so we can talk more closely. "I felt I was being repressed by my foster carers in the girls' home." She scoffs at her own immaturity. "I was compelled to rebel, and Calvin was just the sort of guy they told us to keep away from."

"You were in foster care?"

"From the age of twelve. I never met my father and my mom had her demons."

"Alcohol?"

"Bipolar."

"I'm sorry."

She shrugs. "It seems like we're cut from the same cloth, after all. Shitty parents, rough upbringing. Except you ended up in one type of prison and I in another."

"How did you meet Calvin?"

"I got a fake ID when I was sixteen years old. I used to dress up like the older girls I hung around with, borrow their clothes and make-up, make myself look older. I used to hang around with the wrong crowd, but all that mattered to me was that they treated me like their own. The early years of my life were lonely ones."

I nod. I know that feeling. I spent years locked away in my room, just trying to keep away from my drunken mother and any one of her latest love affairs.

"I was at a bar one night when I met Calvin. His eyes picked me out through the crowd like I was the only girl in the room." She smiles at the memory. "He was nineteen and handsome as sin. He drank like a fish, swore like a sailor, and fucked like a..." She trails off with a mischievous smile that makes me hard.

I know how Megan fucks.

"He bought my drinks that night. We danced to every song. When the bar closed, I got on the back of his motorbike and he drove me around the city. He didn't care that he didn't have a license or that he'd been drinking. Calvin just did what he wanted. It was such a breath of fresh are after growing up...*institutionalized*. There were no rules or restrictions with Calvin. He made me feel as free as a bird."

She hugs her knees and smiles. Whatever happened in the later days, the early ones were obviously good. She loved her own monster once; just like my mother. *At least Megan had the sense to recognize evil in the man in the end.*

"And then?"

Megan laughs. "Like an idiot, I ran away with him. We had a few good, good years when it was just him and me. We went everywhere on that rusty old bike, drinking in every bar we found along the way. We stayed up all night partying. We had sex constantly. We made each day up as it came along, living with no plans. Completely carefree. I was head over heels for him."

"What happened?"

"Calvin had this chip on his shoulder. His own father was some drug lord with a reputation. The day he found out he'd died in a shoot-out, he changed. Calvin suddenly felt like he had to live up to his father's legacy. Instead of just doing weed and the odd line, he wanted to do meth and heroin. Then he got past that; he wanted to sell it instead. He started making money by taking advantage of people's addictions. Then, when he had some money in his bank, he started buying guns. He'd use those guns to get more drugs, and it kept on and on from there."

She pauses to look down at her lap in mournful contemplation, fiddling with the hem of her skirt. "I stayed with him thinking it was just his own strange way of grieving. I thought if enough time passed, he'd find his way back to who he was. But once he got a taste of power, he was addicted. He started gathering followers—the sort of people who always want to be on the stronger side—and it just fed into this ego. Before my eyes, he changed from this carefree rebel into a narcissistic, paranoid monster. Everything I loved about him disappeared."

"Why didn't you leave?"

"I had nowhere to go." Megan's eyes flicker against tears. I can hear the tremble of regret in her voice. "I had no family, no friends outside Calvin's circle, no money. I was scared of ending up on the streets, and despite everything, I depended on Calvin. When I was young and alone, he gave me a home. He showed me love. I couldn't let go of what used to be. He was my world when we were young. And he wasn't always cruel."

"I find that hard to believe."

"It's true." She runs her finger along the bedsheets, lost in her own memories. "Sometimes he was even kind. I mean, Calvin could be hard as hell on me, but if anyone else ever tried to hurt me in any way, he would defend me to the death. It made me feel wanted and loved. It made me forgive him for all the shit he put me through, because who else would love me like he did? Who else would love me at all?"

I reach for her hand and squeeze. "I'd bet there are few people in the world easier to love than you."

She pulls her hand away and sobs. "Don't say that. I don't deserve anybody's love. You were right about me the whole time. I let too many horrible things happen."

"The guilt will eat you alive," I say. "It was only when I was in prison and reflecting on all the ways I fucked up in life that I started to think about all the other ways things could have gone. What if I'd phoned the police years ago? What if I had left and let my mom and that psycho live their hellish lives on their own? He might have beaten her senseless every day, but maybe she'd have still been alive by now. She loved him, as monstrous as he was."

"I'm sorry you had to grow up like that."

"Second best? Fuck that." I clench my jaw. "I didn't matter

to her at all. Or else she would have never brought that man into our home." I clear my throat. "I don't want to talk about her anyway. Saving her life was the worst thing I ever did."

Megan looks up at me with tear-stained eyes. "Worse than saving mine?"

The way she looks at me makes my heart stop. There's gratitude and something more in her eyes; that same affection that drew me toward her in the first place. Somehow, this messed-up woman pierces her way through my own chaos and makes me feel real; human in a way I thought I'd never feel again.

Jesus Christ, I know I love her. It's fast. It's stupid. It's senseless. But this woman makes me feel like there are things left in this world worth fighting for.

"It'll be worth it if you have a good life. Don't be like my mother. You've got a second chance. You've escaped. Be happy."

Megan grasps my hand. "There's still time for you to run. I don't have to mention that you were ever here."

"I'm not leaving you. I believe someone in the FBI is on Calvin's payroll. I can't figure out any other way they'd know where you were. For all I know, that man is Khosa. I'm not leaving you here alone."

There's a moment of silence between us. After a hostile afternoon, Megan finally lets me put my arm around her. She's drained, and so am I. We lean on each other, heads close together, sharing our remorse and our sadness.

"I left it too late to leave him. I was selfish, thinking about what life would be like on my own. And scared—I knew exactly what would happen the day I left him. If he couldn't have me, nobody could. He must have told me that a million times."

"You're testifying against him," I reply. "What's the charge?"

"Murder, among other awful things."

"Did he do it?"

"Of course, he did."

"Did you see it?"

"Yes."

"I'm sorry. You've been through a lot."

"I'm no victim, Jack. Sometimes I wonder if I was as bad as him."

"You're not. I was in prison a long time. Trust me, I know bad people."

MEGAN

"KHOSA WON'T BE LONG NOW."

"It depends where he's coming from."

I'm so tired. All I want to do is sleep. I'm in pieces over nearly dying today, and I'm in pieces over finding out Jack wasn't who he said he was. Even worse, knowing he was out to kill me and still feeling desire every time I look at him.

You were born to self-destruct, Megan.

"Was Calvin ever abusive?" Jack asks me.

I take in a short, sharp breath. "Why does that matter?"

"I'm trying to understand how you stayed with him for so long when you're obviously a good person."

"You don't know what kind of person I am."

"I watched you when you didn't even know I was there. You smile at everyone, friendly and kind. You buy flowers every morning when you get back from the café to brighten up your living room. You surround yourself with beautiful things and only give back beauty. I just can't believe you wanted to be in the situation you were in."

"I told you: I loved him."

"And that's it?"

My eyes well up with tears. Why is Jack pushing it? He's acting like I have to explain myself when he's the one who was contracted to kill me.

"Even if he did hit me, that's not the reason I stayed."

Jack nods. I can tell he thinks he's found the answer—I was an abused, trapped woman. He's wrong. My fear of Calvin was only outweighed by my love for him. It was that love that kept me there far more than fear.

"And you? You would have killed me for $150,000. Would it have been worth it?"

"For a second, I wondered."

"More than a second. You came all the way from Maryland to Illinois, to the café where I was, to talk to me... You thought about it for more than a moment."

"You're right." Jack bows his head in shame. "But that was back when I thought you were some cokehead gangster chick who'd pulled a trigger as many times as her gang lord ex. Once I met you, I realized I couldn't be more wrong."

"So if I had been a violent cokehead, I'd be dead now?"

Jack shrugs. "Jesus, Megan. I don't know. All I know is that I was dealt a shit hand in life. I was raised in an abusive family with a different drunk guy in the house every other week to torment me alongside my equally drunk mother. That is, of course, until she married Donnie, and then it was the same guy beating the hell out of me day after day. All I wanted was to get away and get out of that town. I wanted to go to art school. I *could* have gone to art school. The key was in my hand.

"Then I saw him beating her bloody until she wasn't even screaming anymore, and I did what I had to do to save her life. And what did I get in return? Fourteen years and not so much as a goodbye before she hung herself in the bedroom. Left me alone to rot in there."

He picks at a fingernail with his thumb. "Was I ready to

say fuck everyone else and to start putting myself first? Did I want the money to give myself a chance I never had? Did I think I deserved that chance more than someone who'd sworn herself to a serial killer? Fuck yes, I did. But...here I am. I don't have money or family or much of anything, to be honest, but I have my integrity. I won't die rich or famous, but I'd like to die a good man."

I listen to his story feeling both pity and distrust. He's lied to me so far. How do I know anything he's saying now is true?

I lower my voice to a soft whisper. "Really, Jack, you should go."

"I'm not going anywhere."

"Even if you end up back in prison?"

"I've been out the joint for less than two months and look where I am. I was born in the gutters, and I'll die in the gutters. At least I know my place on the inside."

I want to tell him I love him, but I know that can't be true. We've only known each other days and all the time we spent together was a lie. And yet...I want to protect him. I don't want to think of him spending another lifetime behind bars. I want to save him.

"Come sit with me."

"What?"

I move up against the headboard and pat the mattress at my side. "Sit here."

Jack moves up beside me, settling his back against the faux-leather headboard and stretching his legs out across the mattress. He seems uncomfortable like he doesn't know where the boundaries are anymore. Neither do I.

All I know is that I want to be near him one last time before the world comes crashing down. I've done something stupid. I've betrayed the man who saved my life.

I rest my heavy head against his shoulder and don't pull

away when he wraps his arms around me. I blink and tears roll down my cheeks. I keep my head bowed so Jack doesn't see my crying.

"It's your last chance to run, Jack. They're almost here."

He tightens his hold on me warmly. "I'm not going anywhere."

JACK

So, this is Senior Inspector Khosa.

He is a serious and distinguished looking man with a neatly clipped beard, smart suit, and a ferocious glare that he fixes on me.

He's not alone. Senior Inspector Tom Kroft is with him, standing just a step behind, the junior of the two.

Khosa puts his hand on the grip of his revolver and pulls it from its holster, pointing it at me. "On the ground."

"Khosa, no!" Megan pleas. "Abdel...stop."

The Inspector hesitates when she uses his first name. "Megan, I don't know who this man is. Get behind me."

"He saved me from getting shot."

"I thought this man was contracted to kill you."

I cast a glance across at Megan. I didn't know she'd told him that.

She looks across at me with a guilty expression. "I'm sorry, Jack. I panicked. I messaged him everything when we were on the bus. I wish I hadn't."

"Raise your hands slowly above your head," Khosa instructs. He keeps the gun pointed at me. My stomach sinks, but I don't object. I knew this is what would happen if I chose to stay.

I look across to Megan where she sits safe and alive, and I would do it again.

Khosa makes eye contact with Kroft and jerks his head toward me. Tom moves toward where I sit on the bed, extending a pair of handcuffs in front of him.

"Stand up and turn around," Khosa commands.

I do as I'm told, standing up from the bed and turning to face the drawn drapes. Tom is rough when he grabs me by the wrists and puts me in iron. I'm used to the feeling of them now. I feel sick when I hear them clicking into place. Fourteen years of hell behind me, only for it all to start again. I'm weak at the knees with despair. My whole life...it's destined to be wasted behind bars.

You've only got yourself to blame, Jack. You took the offer.

"Please," Megan begs. "He's the only reason I'm here. He hasn't hurt me in the slightest."

"Are you sure?" Tom responds. "Those look like some pretty nasty bruises on your wrists."

Megan looks down to the purple imprints of my fingers from where I dragged her through the streets this morning.

"He was pulling me after him to get me away from the hitman. He was saving my life."

"This man is an assassin."

Megan stands up defiantly, her fists clenched at her sides and her eyes wet with tears. "Jack was there when someone shot at me this morning. Where were you?"

I can't see Khosa as I'm still facing the window, but I can sense his seething rage at the accusation.

"I understand you're emotional right now, but I have to follow protocol. Whether he saved your life or not, this man has a lot of explaining to do."

Tom takes hold of my shoulder and spins me around so

I'm facing the room again. I meet Megan's eyes. She looks beside herself with guilt. Even though I'm in cuffs and prepared for another trial and conviction, it feels good to see that sorrow in her eyes. *She cares.*

"It's okay, Megan," I say. "This isn't your fault."

Pushing down on my shoulder, Tom presses me back down onto the bed. When I am sitting, he takes Megan by the elbow to lead her out the room.

Megan resists. "Where are we going?"

"I'm taking you to a squad car outside. We're going to take you to a safe house in the city."

"I don't want to go. I want to stay with Jack."

"Ma'am, this man is a convicted killer. Do you have any idea who Jack Woodson is?"

She catches my eye with a tearful gaze. "He's the man who came back for me."

"He's a snake in the grass. Come with me, Miss Cartwright. I'm going to get you somewhere safe. If this man is as innocent as you say he is, then he'll be out in no time. For now, we need to ask him some questions to figure out exactly what went on here."

Megan is torn away, and Khosa and I are left alone in the room.

Khosa keeps a few steps' distance, staring at me with pure repulsion. "Tell me what happened. Everything. Leave nothing out."

So I do. I tell him everything. I leave nothing out.

When I'm finished, Khosa kneels in front of me; he comes real close until we're practically nose to nose.

"You'd better thank God you didn't pull the trigger on that girl or this conversation would be going very differently right now."

"I couldn't hurt her."

"Anyone who does will have me to answer to."

Clearly, I'm not the only one under Megan's spell. She's an innocent child caught in a web of bad decisions that left her in the midst of chaos. She isn't a bad person. I know it, and so does Khosa.

"You're a piece of shit for even thinking of hurting her." Khosa goes to the bedside table where he'd deposited a portfolio of documents when he first entered. He picks up the folder and throws it down beside me. He points at it. "I've read all about you, Mr. Woodson. Killed your stepfather with a bowling ball. You're clearly one for drama. A bit of a showman, are we? Dodging bullets, taking buses across the county, smashing in people's skulls...Give you a rush, does it?"

The cuffs are digging into my wrists, uncomfortable, but it's Khosa who's really getting under my skin.

"I know what I am. You're right: I'm a piece of shit for even considering harming her. But I didn't."

"Then why have you been following her, huh? Why does she turn up here with you? If you'd walked away from the deal, why am I even talking to your sorry ass right now?"

"Someone else would have come."

"You know that, do you? You know what Calvin's up to?"

"Today was the first time I'd ever heard his name."

"Ah yes, three degrees of separation." He flicks back through his notepad in which he was taking notes while I was speaking. "You got given the contract by 'Sparky,' that right? And what's his real name?"

"Charlie. I don't know his surname."

"Your cell mate for fourteen years and you expect me to believe you don't know his surname?"

"Not a fucking clue. But I can do you one better."

"Oh yeah?"

"I know his address. His cell number. His pant size. I can give you anything you need."

"Not one for loyalty, are we?"

"As long as Sparky's out there, he's making plans to hurt Megan."

"And why should you care so much?" He fixes his hard glare on me and then chuckles. "Got a little crush, have we? I wouldn't get your hopes up too much. Assassin and victim isn't a classic love story."

"She knows I'd never hurt her."

"Are you sure?" Khosa pulls out his cell and starts to read from a message. "On the 13:05 greyhound bus from Galena to Chicago. Someone tried to shoot me this morning. I'm with a man named Jack Goodson who saved me, but I don't trust him. He says he was the one who was first contracted to kill me. Please send help."

I wince. The words hurt. I thought Megan trusted me. I close my eyes and think of the pain in her eyes when Tom pulled her away. She regretted naming me. I know she did.

"If I was going to hurt her, then why did I stay here and wait for you to arrive? Why didn't I run and save myself?"

"Maybe you've got someone to fear more than me. Instructions from the top dog, so to speak."

"I've never met Calvin Raynor."

"Alright. Well, tell me something you do know."

"Like what?"

"How did Calvin, or Sparky, or whoever the fuck gave you that paperwork, know where to find Megan?"

"Sparky said something about an insider at WITSEC. That's why I've stayed with her. Someone on your team is dirty."

Khosa paces around the room. "I bet I know who."

"You do?"

"Mugawny. He's a sleazy bastard. I've never trusted him. An accusation was made against him about a year ago about breaching confidentiality. He left a folder on a train. It was determined it was accidental, and he was back on the team after a three-month suspension. My guess is it wasn't an accident at all. I'd bet that Megan's file was left on a train just the same for someone to pick up and pass along."

Khosa stands with a hand on his hip and looks back over his shoulder at me. "Get up. We're going to the station."

* * *

Seven hours with nothing but a bottle of water and a flickering fluorescent light in a concrete room with my hands shackled to the table. I've been here before, a long time ago. I know how it goes. They'll ask you the same questions over and over until you break and change your story just to get out of the room.

I've told my story again and again at least a dozen times today. Hours of testimony. A confession that's lasted all evening and into the early hours of the next morning. It must be 3 a.m. by now.

I'm exhausted and worried about Megan. Nobody will tell me anything about where she is or whether she's safe. I don't trust these men to protect her. They've already failed once.

The door opens. I look up to see which of the suited fed-bots has come to interrogate me now.

It's Tom Kroft. He's only in his thirties, a greenhorn in the federal agency. He has chestnut brown hair neatly cropped like a soldier and a tie that's in a knot that looks like it was measured with a ruler. He sure looks the part.

"How much longer will I be in this room?" I ask. "If I'm being charged, charge me. Take me to prison for Christ's sake. Just let me out of this god-damned interrogation room."

"Khosa would like to charge you," Tom says casually. "He'd like you hung, drawn, and quartered, in fact, but I've managed to convince him that we've got better uses for you."

Good cop, bad cop.

"Oh yeah?"

"That we have bigger fish to fry. Calvin Raynor."

"I told you—I've never met the man."

"Still, you're a valuable witness for the state. I'm willing to offer you a deal."

"...Okay."

"After all, you didn't pull the trigger on Megan Cartwright. In fact, you got her to safety and have cooperated with federal investigators. If you continue to cooperate, then maybe we can help each other."

"What do you want from me?"

"Your testimony, in court. We have Megan's, but Raynor's trial is a big one. If we get him, we bring down the head of a whole crime organization. We can halve Baltimore's crime rate overnight. That's worth more than holding onto some would-be assassin with daddy-issues."

"Donnie wasn't my father."

"He wasn't anybody's anything after you smashed his head in with that bowling ball."

"I want full immunity."

"Full immunity? You agreed to assassinate a woman."

"Can you prove that?"

"Your own testimony."

"Well, maybe I want to retract my statement and change my story. Everything you've got me on is circumstantial."

Kroft draws in a deep, slow, breath. "You're lucky that tens of thousands of police hours have gone into the Raynor case. You have a deal. You testify, you're off the hook." He reaches forward to unlock my chains. "We're taking you into witness protection to make sure you're still alive by the time the trial rolls around."

I laugh. "Are you kidding me?"

"This is serious, Jack. You know as well as anyone that Raynor has his means."

"And Megan?"

"She's safe."

"Can I see her?"

"You'll never see her again, and you should be kissing my feet that it's ended that way. You're getting off scot-free for a very serious crime. Maybe try and keep the body count down to one in this lifetime, huh? No more hits, Mr. Woodson. Keep your nose clean, and you may well have a shot at a half-decent life—even if it is more than you deserve."

MEGAN

SIX MONTHS later

The District Court of Maryland is a modern building; nothing like what they show you in the movies. There are no pillars or marble steps. The building is plain white brick with simple silver letters to identify it. It's not even that big.

But this is where it's happening. This is where I'm going to face Calvin once again. The prosecutors wanted me to give video testimony for my own sake, but I wanted to look Calvin in the eye when I described every vile thing I'd ever seen him do; when I described how he killed a boy who was barely more than a child.

And more than that...I want to see Jack. I don't know if he'll be there, but I'm hoping against hope he will be. After all, he's part of Calvin's saga now, too.

My stomach is a ball of nerves as I walk toward the entrance, surrounded by lawyers and federal agents. For the last six months I've been living as Lisa Goody in Minnesota, and stepping back into Baltimore feels like seeing the sun for the first time in forever. As soon as Calvin is behind bars, I know I'll be breathing free air again.

If Calvin ends up behind bars.

I shudder at the thought, but I know it's possible that despite everyone's best preparations, Calvin might get away. He has connections and has already killed off two witnesses.

Khosa and Kroft refused to tell me anything about Jack after he was arrested in the hotel room. I don't know where he is, what he was charged with, or whether I'll ever see him again. I'm praying this courtroom reunites us.

I've had months to think. All I want is to look him in the eye and tell him I'm sorry. If a monster like me deserved to be saved, then a hero like Jack deserves all the good things life can bring. God knows he was one of the only good things life brought me.

Carla Resotti keeps pace beside me, marching at a hundred miles per hour toward the courthouse in her patent leather shoes with her armful of documents. She's the lead prosecutor in this case, and even though I've run through my testimony a thousand times with her, she's still drilling last-minute advice into me.

"It's okay to be afraid. In fact, it's great if you show that fear. Calvin's a monster, and the world needs to know it.

"If you need time, take it. You can wait as long as you need to between answers. Take the time to gather your thoughts and remember things as they happened. Remember, you have total immunity, so you can drag Calvin through the mud even if it makes you look bad. Don't worry what the jury thinks of you—you're not the one on trial."

I can't help but worry. If I'm as honest as Carla wants me to be, then a jury of my peers is going to judge me as a disgrace to humankind, let off only by a loophole that let me free because there was a bigger devil to take down.

"They'll try to make you look bad. It doesn't matter how bad you look as long as Calvin looks every bit as guilty."

Carla has a habit of making me feel like a criminal, too.

She is always reminding me that it's okay if I've done terrible things or let terrible things happen, as long as I shed light on Calvin's darkness. Except...it does matter. It does matter that I was a witness who didn't speak until it was far too late.

I hold up my hand. "Please, Carla. My head is pounding. Can I just take this time to calm my nerves and think?"

She smiles and nods, giving my shoulder a quick squeeze. "Sure thing, darling. I'm here if you need me. Not that you will. I know you'll smash this trial. You want to take Calvin down as much as anyone."

Any love I had for Calvin is gone after the last six months. Time in solitude has made me realize how fucked up our relationship was. Jack—a complete stranger—would risk his own freedom to save my life. Calvin was willing to stomp my self-esteem into shreds and try to control the broken pieces of what was left.

I'm ready to let go of him, his evil, and all I've seen and done. This is the day of my redemption and Calvin's downfall.

As I'm giving myself a pep talk in my head, I look up and all the rehearsed words fall from my mind.

It's Jack.

Healthy and well, there he stands. He's grown a short beard, and he's wearing a smart button-up shirt with dress pants. He's even got on a slim gray tie and cufflinks. He looks every bit the gentleman I believed him to be when I first met him in that café back in Illinois. His tattoos don't show, nor does the darkness that haunted him when I knew him before. He looks rejuvenated.

He spots me too, and his face lights up. He tears away from his own gaggle of lawyers and jogs across the courthouse foyer to hug me.

"Megan." He stands back to look me up and down. "Thank God you're safe. I was hoping to see you here."

I place my hand over his where it rests on my shoulder. "I was too."

"How have you been?" he asks me.

"You mean who have I been?"

He chuckles. "Another new life?"

"Yes. How about you?"

"Isn't the beard enough? I thought I was indistinguishable from my old self."

I smile. "It suits you." Looking at him, I feel old desires flaring. That old, familiar sense of safety and comfort I felt the first time Jack was nearby and ever since floods over me once again. "Is it too much to say I've missed you?"

"Because we only knew each other a few days and then you found out I was sent to murder you?" Jack smiles wryly. "No, I don't think so." He steps forward and kisses my forehead. "I missed you too."

"What the hell do you think you're doing?"

It's Khosa. He steps in between Jack and me, grabs my shoulder and protectively pulls me away from him.

"You two should be nowhere near each other. You're both in witness protection. You shouldn't even recognize each other." He glances at Jack. "And I still don't trust you."

"I've stayed put where you sent me," Jack says defensively. "I've left Megan alone. As you told me."

"Don't say her name, you moron." Khosa casts his gaze around the foyer. "You never know who's listening, and it's never too late for Calvin to try one last Hail Mary."

Khosa looks up for his partner and clicks his fingers to get the attention of Kroft, who's standing with a coffee about twenty feet away. "Kroft, get her out of here."

Tom looks up and quickly assesses the situation. He abandons his coffee on a windowsill and obediently comes to take me out of the foyer, another state prosecutor ushers Jack away.

I smile. Jack is alive and well, and any day, any *hour* now, Calvin will get what's coming to him.

After that, I have plans to see Jack again. He's the only thing I can ever think about these days. I want to give us a shot at something real. If we hadn't met during this bullshit game of spies, I believe real love could have blossomed—and we both deserve to be truly loved at last.

JACK

I SIT with spectators and journalists in the pews as Megan takes the stand. She's incredibly brave. She steps up with a straight back and steady step, and I watch in admiration as she takes her seat and makes a point to meet Calvin's eye, lifting her chin in defiance.

Finally, I get to see the man who entrapped Megan and tried to hire me to take her life. He doesn't look like the lowlife I imagined. In his suit, with his dark hair cut into an expensive neat style, sitting with the posture of a monarch, he looks like part of upper-crust society, not a gangster.

I hope the jury sees right through him.

He is expressionless throughout Megan's testimony. The only change on his face is a smirk when Megan tears up reliving the murder she witnessed. His smugness gets under her skin. I can see her closing up, losing her voice.

I clear my throat loudly. She looks up and spots me in the crowd. I hold my gaze and nod. *You can do this.*

She draws in a shuddering breath and continues with her testimony. I'm proud of her. Megan didn't let me down. I saved her, and she rose like a phoenix to defy the odds stacked against her and turn away from her former life.

Calvin's smirk disappears when he realizes he can't intimidate her.

When Megan finally steps down from the stand, she looks vindicated; empowered. I wish I could run down the aisle, pick her up, spin her around, and tell her how incredible she is. Instead, I have to sit silently in the pews while more evidence is unveiled.

Murder, kidnap, assault...This guy is the lowest of the low.

Finally, it's my turn to testify. Megan didn't falter, and neither will I.

I step up onto the stand, swear to tell the truth, and stare that bastard straight in the eye. I'm not sure he even knows who I am.

"Mr. Goodson, in July of last year you were told about a 'job' offered to you by the defendant. Would you care to tell the court what that job entailed?"

"I was asked to kill Miss Megan Cartwright."

"To kill her?"

"Yes."

"And what were the terms of this contract."

"I would be paid $150,000."

"And you accepted this offer?"

"I did."

The jury gasps, tuts and shake their heads. I can see the disgust on their faces; it's a mirror for the disgust I've felt for myself. I take a deep breath and let the feeling go. While I've been living my life as Colin Meyers, I've had time to evaluate my life and the choices I've made. I decided to forgive myself. *I am not an evil man.*

"And what happened next?"

"I received a dossier on Megan Cartwright."

Carla lifts the folder I'd passed onto her. "Please note Evidence Item 3E."

She puts the folder on the stand in front of me and asks me to read out select passages which specify Megan as the target, instructions to kill her and to show the jury her photograph.

I look up over the document to find Megan in the crowd. She must hate me, knowing I read this file and chose to hunt her down.

When I find her in the crowd, there are tears running down her face, but she doesn't look away when I catch her eye. She smiles to reassure me and returns the same encouraging nod I offered her.

I continue, telling the court everything that happened.

"And after you refused to carry out the contract, what happened?"

"Someone else tried to kill Megan."

The story unfolds piece by piece as I tell the jury all about my role in Megan's assassination attempt. It all leads back to Calvin—the evil mastermind who uses other people's hands to carry out his sickening crimes.

I feel like everything's going well—until the defense rises to cross-examine me.

"Mr. Goodson, it's true this is the first time you have ever laid eyes on Calvin Raynor in the flesh?"

"It's true."

"So how do you know it was he who gave the order for you to carry out this assassination?"

"I know. I was told the instructions were coming from Megan's ex."

"Can you know for sure that that's the truth of the matter?"

"I believe it was the truth."

"How can you be sure?"

"Who else would want to kill her? She's an incredible woman."

"Conjecture." The defense lawyer raises his eyebrows smugly. "The truth is, Mr. Goodson, you have no idea who wanted you to kill Megan Cartwright, and you didn't care. You have no way of knowing it was my client who gave the order for you to kill Miss Cartwright. Furthermore, no money ever exchanged hands—is that correct? There is no evidence of any crime at all."

* * *

Three days of testimony, evidence, and interrogation. Now we're at the end of an eight-hour wait for the jury's verdict.

Khosa has tried to keep me behind closed doors while we wait, but as soon as he excuses himself to the restroom, I slip out the door of the conference room where we're waiting and escape into the foyer.

The risk pays off—Megan and Carla are standing at a vending machine getting another batch of coffee.

Carla sees me approaching and frowns. "You two should be nowhere near each other. You know that."

"Five minutes, Carla. Please," Megan begs. "You know Khosa will tear us apart the second he reappears."

Carla fixes me with a hard stare. "I'm going to turn a blind eye for *five minutes* and only because this girl told me what you did for her." She turns to Megan. "I'm only going to be six feet away. I don't want you to leave this foyer. Understand me?"

"I understand."

She steps away, and Megan and I grin at each other like naughty school children. She throws her arms around me and hugs me tighter than I've ever been hugged.

"Jack, it's so good to see you."

"Is it really? I didn't think you'd be able to bear to look at me again after what you heard in court today."

"Weren't you listening to my testimony? I thought you'd be disgusted by the things I've done."

"The things you've witnessed. There's a difference."

"Carla, Khosa, everyone...they say I'm mad to trust you."

"Maybe you are."

"I can't help it, Jack. Somewhere between the lies and disguise, I think there was a real connection. Everything you told me about your mother and your stepfather—it was all true?"

"Every word."

"And you really did want to go to art school?"

"I had the scholarship, just like I said." I smile teasingly. "And you really do like cheese and horror movies?"

"I swear to God."

"Megan, I need to tell you how sorry I am. I never did." I bow my head and take both her hands in mine. "I had a moral lapse that almost led to me doing the worst thing I ever did in my life. I want you to know that I've used the time I've had away to take a long hard look at myself. I meditate now. I read a self-help book a day. I swear I've been trying to tap into the best part of me and make it"—I spread my hands apart meaningfully—"*bigger*."

"I'm sorry, too. I turned you in. I was scared. I didn't know. Then once we got to the hotel room and the adrenaline wore off, and we started talking, I realized you weren't lying to me. You had a momentary lapse of judgment. I forgive you."

"Can you really forgive someone for something like that?"

"Could Aiden's family ever forgive me for letting their son, their brother, die?" Megan shakes her head slowly. "Sometimes even the unforgivable can be forgiven. I may not like the choices you made, but god damned if I haven't made similar ones myself. I forgive you, Jack."

A weight is lifted off my shoulders. I don't think anyone's forgiven me before. Is this it? Have I achieved redemption? Is there a happy future for me in sight?

"You're a good woman, Megan." I look around at the flock of prosecutors and security. "I wish we could get out of here. We should slip out to a coffee shop or something, and you can tell me all about whose life you're living these days."

Megan laughs but shakes her head. "I've learned to live like the walls have ears. Khosa probably has eyes on me right now. Besides, I want to be here when the verdict is read."

I grip her shoulder. "He's going away."

She bites down on her lip and looks up at me with fearful eyes. "I have this feeling like it won't be that easy."

"Trust me. You're safe."

"I haven't felt safe since the day we went our separate ways in that hotel room." She twists the toe of her shoes into the floor. "I miss you."

"I miss you, too."

"When all this is over, do you think maybe you and I could see each other again? As unconventional and terrifying and wrong as it may be?"

"More than anything, I hope that's exactly what happens."

"Step away from each other!"

We step apart and both roll our eyes. Khosa has found us. He grabs me roughly by the shoulder and pulls me away.

"Jesus Christ, do I need to put an ankle tag on you? Stay where I put you, for God's sake."

MEGAN

WE GATHER AGAIN in the courtroom for the verdict to be heard. The room is stuffed full of reporters, artists, and TV journalists.

The energy and tension in the room are palpable. I'm holding my breath waiting to hear what is decided. The jury files in, the judge sits, and he asks Calvin to stand.

"Calvin Raynor, you stand accused of two counts of murder, six counts of illegal possession of a firearm, one count of assault, and one count of kidnapping." He turns to the jury. "How do you find the defendant."

I'm holding my breath so hard I think I might faint. I grip onto the pew in front of me to stop myself falling out of my seat. I twist my neck to find Jack in the crowd. He's flanked by Kroft and Khosa, but he's searching for me too.

"It's okay," he mouths.

I turn back to the jury. They're a mixed bunch—young, old, men, women, Caucasian, Hispanic, African-American. There's no bias here. I pray the facts speak for themselves. I pray I haven't put myself through this in vain.

Please let him go down.

A spokesman stands up. He's a middle-aged man with a bald head but a full mustache. He clears his throat, reading from a cue card in his hand.

"We, the jury, unanimously find the defendant, Calvin Raynor, guilty on all charges."

The judge thanks them and turns back to Calvin.

"Mr. Raynor, throughout this trial this court has heard how you killed, tortured, and assaulted indiscriminately and repeatedly for your own gain. We've heard how you kidnapped a young man, held him against his will, and eventually took his life. There seems to be no low you have not sunk to. Drugs, firearms, murder, and domestic abuse paint a picture of just a fraction of your tyranny. It is the opinion of this court that you are a danger to society, and I have no doubts that if we were to let you leave today, you'd be back to your old ways within the hour. You have a long and persistent history of brutal and violent crime, against strangers, and against those you claimed to care for. I hereby sentence you to three consecutive life terms without parole for these crimes of which you have been convicted. Do you have anything to say before your sentence begins?"

As soon as Calvin turns to face the spectators, I know there will be no apology, no remorse, no final pleas of innocence.

Instead, he finds me in the crowd and kisses at me. "You got lucky, sweetheart. Next time I'll send someone more experienced to hunt you down."

The judge draws back his lips in a scowl. "Take him away."

And just like that, the worst part of my life is lead away in shackles as my own are released. *I'm free.*

I don't care what the rules are. I don't care what Khosa might say. I push my way out of the pew and to the aisle and wait for Jack to make his own way to the middle of the room. I throw my arms around him and kiss him joyously.

"We did it, Jack! He's behind bars. For good."

Jack wraps his arms around me, picks me up, and spins me right there in the courtroom. My laughter rings around the room. I know I'm being filmed; I know this will be in the papers. But who cares? There's nothing to stop me now.

Khosa tries to pull Jack away, but I step between them. "Come on now, Abdel. The trial is over."

"You never know what kind of revenge Calvin might have planned."

"I'm done with living in fear. Fuck Calvin."

I turn back to Jack and kiss him again. He's laughing; I'm crying. We're both overwhelmed with the joy in our newfound freedom and in the relief that we've both risen from the ashes of criminal lives.

I hold Jack's face between my hands. "I'm going to live like a saint starting today."

"I'm ready for picnics and walks on the beach and cooking classes and all that normal shit. I'm ready for an ordinary, happy life."

I can't let go of him. Every time I try to draw myself away, the magnetism of my feelings for him pulls me back. Who knows how much of what I feel is gratitude and adrenaline? Who knows how much is love?

All I know is that I've missed Jack with everything in me, and every night I've had fantasies of being back in his arms. In him, I've found a kindred spirit; someone who's walked the same path and had the same epiphany, the same desire to reinvent themselves and be made whole again. I feel whole with him.

Jack takes my hand. We walk down the middle aisle like a newlywed couple, big matching grins on our faces. Outside, the journalists swarm us, asking for our statements.

Calvin seems to have been forgotten. There's one question every reporter is burning to ask.

"Miss Cartwright! Miss Cartwright! How would you describe your current relationship with Mr. Goodson? Isn't it true he tried to take your life?"

"He saved my life." I turn to face the cameras. "For anyone out there who's done bad things, look at us. Redemption is possible. Walk away from what you're doing and choose to be better. It's hard, but today justice has been done and an evil man is behind bars. It's possible to start again."

JACK

"JACK. *JACK!*" Khosa calls out to me, running after me once I'm outside the court. "Where the hell do you think you're going?"

"With Megan."

"Are you crazy? You're both in the witness protection program."

"I'm opting out."

"Excuse me?"

"I'm opting out of the program."

"We still don't know how far Calvin's reach goes."

"I don't care. I have a life to live."

"And where are you planning to go?"

One glance at Megan is all it takes for him to read my intentions. "Like I'm going to let you follow her into her new life. She's doing well. She's safe. If anyone's on your tail, you're going to lead them straight to her."

"Consider it two for the price of one."

"You're not in love, Goodson."

"No?"

"No. You're deluded. You're a criminal."

"I was never a criminal, and I'm still not. The only thing I regret in my life is putting my mother's life before my own."

"You don't regret agreeing to murder the woman you think you're in love with?"

"If I hadn't been the one who was sent first, she'd be dead by now."

"She had protection."

"No. She didn't."

It's chaos just outside the courthouse. I can hear snippets of news reports from every direction as more journalists try to get to the lawyers, to Megan, to me. I reach out to Megan, and she takes my hand. I grip onto her for dear life.

Megan leans against me and smiles up at Khosa.

"Abdel, it's alright. It's over."

"I can't allow you two to leave together."

"Then I opt out too."

"What?"

"I'm out of the program. It's my choice. You said so yourself."

"If you leave the program, I can't protect you."

"That's okay. I know someone who can." She looks up at me, beaming. I feel more of a man than I've ever felt. Megan trusts me to protect her—and I was born to be a protector. It's the only thing I've ever been good at.

"She's right, Khosa. I'll take care of her, I swear." I slap him on the shoulder like we're old friends, which pisses him off. He brushes off his arm like I've tagged him with the plague virus. "And if anything seems off, we'll give you a call."

"I won't stand for it. Stay here a moment."

Megan chuckles. "Where do you think he's going?"

"Probably to go through my files to find another reason to arrest me." I put my arm around her and pull her close. "He has a thing for you, you know."

She pulls a face and buries her head in my shoulder. "Don't!"

"You know it's true."

"He's a sweet man."

"He hates me."

"He doesn't have to like you. This is my choice."

I step back to look at her. "He's right, you know. We're in more danger together than apart."

"That wasn't true the first time you saved me." She reaches up and places a soft hand on my cheek. Her expression is filled with affection. Her hair is longer now and a paler shade of blonde; it has a slight wave to it. In the winter's sun, she looks angelic. "I've not been able to sleep since we've been apart. Every time there's a loud sound, I think it's a bullet and find myself reaching out for you. But you're not there." She looks up at me pleadingly. "I need you, Jack. Please stay with me."

"You'd really accept me? After all I've done?"

"We've already spoken about this. Neither of us is completely innocent, neither of us is evil. Let's not judge each other. Let's forget who we were and start again."

Khosa returns and slaps my ID into my hand. "Alright, *Colin*. You're going to Minnesota."

"What's in Minnesota?"

Megan beams. "I am."

My eyes widen. "What does this mean?"

"It means I'm not willing to let Megan chase you into the danger zone. If you refuse to be apart, then I guess I'll have to take you both into witness protection."

Megan squeals in excitement and squeezes my hand. She hops up and down in joy. "You're going to love it, Jack! It's beautiful and wholesome, and I have a job now."

"So does Colin."

"You do?"

I smile. "I'm a carpenter now."

"I'm an assistant manager at a bath bomb store."

I throw my head back to laugh. "Who'd have thought, hey? You and I, just ordinary folk."

"We're going to have a good life together."

Khosa rolls his eyes. "Enough, lovebirds. Get in the car. I don't want either of you in this town longer than you need to be."

Megan gets in the car, but as I duck down to follow her, Khosa grabs my arm and pulls me back.

He grunts in my ear. "I'm trusting you to take care of her."

"I'll protect her. With my life." I grip his shoulder and look into his eyes. "You're a good agent, Khosa. And a good man. Thank you for keeping her safe so far. Now it's my turn."

I get in the car and sit beside Megan. We're alone in the back passenger seats. A black screen separates us from the driver who's a federal agent.

We use the time creatively. As soon as the door is shut behind us, I pull Megan toward me and kiss her with all the passion that I've been holding onto over the last six months. She sighs and melts into my kiss.

"This is really happening," she says breathlessly. "We're really starting again. Together."

MEGAN

IT'S MADNESS. Of all the people I should be riding off into the sunset with right now, Jack makes the least sense. I hardly know him, he's lied to me, and I haven't seen him for six months. But every time I'm near him, I feel both fire and honey. There's a passionate, raging storm that wants him and *needs* him; that's hungry for him...but at the same time, there's a sense of safety, comfort, and contentment that makes me feel I'm right where I should be. Fire and honey.

"I can finally tell you who I've been living as," Jack tells me. He pulls out his wallet and shows me his driving license. "Colin Meyers, thirty-four."

I take his ID and look down at his photograph. "Wyoming? So, that's where you've been. And how has life been treating you in the Cowboy State?"

"Surprisingly, I found my feet pretty past. I've enjoyed learning a trade. Carpentry. I thought it was about time I started building things instead of watching them fall apart." He puts his arm around me and sits back with a contented smile. "My first project when we get to wherever we're going will be to build us a love seat."

"A love seat?"

"Just big enough for two, carved beautifully. Maybe I'll set it on a swing for the porch. Does your place have a porch?"

"It doesn't."

"Maybe the next place will."

"Who says you're moving in with me?"

Jack's eyes widen as he backtracks. "I've got means now. We'll live close by."

I laugh and squeeze his hand. "I'm joking. I want you as close as possible. It's going to be good to feel safe again."

I nestle against his chest and close my eyes happily. The space above his collarbone seems to have been molded for my head to rest against. It's so comfortable. I can hear his heart beating while my arms are wrapped around his waist; I can feel his chin resting against my hair. I feel all wrapped up and warm.

"We'll do things however you want them, Megan. I want to start this right."

I raise my head and smile. "It's 'Lucy' now."

"Lucy?"

"Lucy Goody."

Jack makes a face. "Are you kidding me?"

"I know." I chuckle.

"There are ways to change your last name, you know."

"And I thought I was the one letting things happen too quickly."

"I'm excited at the thought of a new, better life, that's all."

"Me, too."

"Speaking of, where is this new life going to take us? Where is home for Lucy Goody?"

"Red Wing, Minnesota."

"The land of ten thousand lakes?"

"I've not seen any of them yet."

"No?"

"I wanted someone to see them with."

I've never been this slushy before, but the dreams and desires are spilling from my lips without restriction. I've held my hopes inside for such a long time, and I'm finally free to let them out; give them life.

Jack feels the same. Like me, he's had a life that's made him into the kind of person he never wanted to be. We've both been prisoners to our bad choices, and now we finally have the chance to do it right.

"We're going to see a lot of things together. I promise you that." He pulls me closer and kisses my forehead. "All good things."

I'm looking out the window as Jack and I cuddle, and I frown when I see us drive right past the exit to the airport.

I twist to look up at Jack. "We just missed the exit to the airport."

"We did?"

"It was back there."

Jack looks out the window and sees the exit disappearing behind us. He leans forward and knocks on the divide between the passengers and driver.

"Excuse me? I think you missed the exit back there."

There's no response. Jack knocks again, louder. But still nothing.

He leans back in his seat and shrugs. "Maybe he knows another way."

"Why doesn't he answer you, then? There's no way he didn't hear you knocking just then."

"I wouldn't worry about it. We'll be on our way to Minnesota soon enough."

Jack doesn't seem perturbed and keeps on talking about all the wonderful things waiting for us in our new life, but I'm uneasy. I haven't seen the driver's face since getting in the car. Khosa is far behind us back in the city. Whoever is sitting in front of us is deliberately ignoring our attempts to get their attention, and we're not heading toward the destination I expected.

Maybe I'm simply paranoid after the last few years of panic and drama, but it doesn't sit right with me.

I cling onto Jack's arm. "I don't like this. I want to know where we're going."

He nods and knocks again. "Excuse me. I said *excuse me*." He balls his hand into a fist and starts slamming it against the divide. "What's your problem? We need to speak to you."

Nothing.

Panic starts to churn in my stomach, making me feel sick. I huddle against Jack until I'm practically on his lap and my mouth goes dry. "Something's wrong."

Jack cuddles me. "Nothing's wrong. Maybe he's got earphones in or something."

"Abdel said Tom would be accompanying us. Have you seen Tom?"

"Kroft? I didn't see the driver. I just got in the car."

"I didn't see either."

He strokes my hair back and gives my lips a soft kiss. Meeting my eyes, he offers me a gentle and reassuring smile. His hands are either side of my face now, softly forcing me to meet his eyes so he can share a look that asks me to trust him.

"I don't blame you for being nervous, Megan, but there's no reason for anyone to be after us now. The trial is over. What's done is done."

"You don't know how vicious Calvin can be. He believes in revenge for revenge's sake, even if it doesn't achieve anything. He just wants you to know he's still won."

"He's in prison, and that's where he's going to stay for a long time. He's won nothing."

I sit up straighter. We've pulled off the highway, heading

into a part of town that looks menacing. The buildings are shabby and covered in graffiti; half of them seem abandoned. I'm in a world of broken glass and boarded up windows.

"Look out the window, Jack," I whisper. "Does this look like a shortcut to the airport to you?"

I see the worry forming in his brow. Jack frowns and pushes me back with an arm across my chest so I'm not visible through the window.

"You're right. There's no reason for us to be this far off the highway. Maybe there's a problem with the car."

"There's nothing wrong with the car."

This is a setup. I can feel it in my bones, a feeling of dread that shudders upward through my body every time the tires roll over a broken bottle or smash into a pothole. We're being taken somewhere dark and distant when WITSEC should be doing everything in their power to keep us safe.

"Maybe they've had intel saying there are eyes on the airport," Jack suggests. "If you were Calvin, isn't there where you'd send your guys? You know the first thing witness protection would do is get the witnesses the hell out of the state. Maybe we're detouring because the airport isn't an option anymore."

"Then why not answer when we knock?" I plead with him with my eyes. "Jack, something bad is about to happen."

Jack licks his lips. They've paled, a sign that maybe he's not as calm as he seems. When he speaks, I hear gravel in his voice.

"I'm not going to let anything happen to you." He leans toward the window, glancing up and down the street. His hand is on the door handle. "We're slowing down. When I tell you to, you're going to get out of the car and run. Keep low. I'll be right behind you."

"You want me to get out the car?"

"We'll find somewhere to lay low until you can call Khosa. You trust him, right?"

"Absolutely."

"I do, too. Better to be safe than sorry. Let's make a run for it."

My heart is beating so fast that I can hardly draw in breaths and my vision is starting to swim. *I thought I was done with all this.*

I slide over to the other side of the car and curl my hand around the door handle. Jack is positioned on the other passenger side. He catches my eye and nods.

"On three. One, two, three."

I tug at the handle, expecting to throw the door open and run. But...the door doesn't budge. The safety lock is on. It's automated, and there's nothing I can do.

Jack swallows and takes a moment to think. "It makes sense for the doors to be locked in a protective vehicle."

"Stop trying to calm me down, Jack. I know we're in danger."

"Call Khosa now."

I do as I'm told. Khosa picks up on the first ring.

"Megan—where are you?" His voice is sharp and intense.

"I don't know. The driver missed the airport exit. He's taken us into a rough-looking part of town. I don't know where we are."

"Whoever is driving that vehicle is *not* our driver. He was found behind the courthouse with a head wound. Looked like he'd been knocked over the back of the head with something. You're in danger, Megan."

My eyes brim with tears. "I knew it."

"Keep your cell on. We have a team trying to locate you. Stay calm and do exactly as you're told by whoever has taken you. Try to buy time while we find out where you are. Help is coming."

I lift my eyes to Jack. In the quiet back seats, he's heard everything. His face is solemn and ashen. The car slows to a stop.

"We're stopping, Abdel. I need to hide the cell. Don't say anything." I throw my cell under the driver's seat and pray nobody at the end of the line makes a sound.

The door slams. I grip Jack's hand. "Did you hear that?"

"The driver got out." He's poised ready to fight. "Everything's going to be okay. Stay alert and follow my lead."

My heart can't cope with the quick leap from joy to terror; I feel it's about to give out any moment. I lay a hand over my chest to try and stop it from pounding so hard. Fresh sweat dampens my forehead.

Jack looks tense and vigilant. Every one of his muscles is taut and prepared for battle. I can see the bulge of them tight beneath his shirt. Unlike my quick, shallow breaths, Jack hardly seems to be breathing at all. He's like a tiger hunting prey.

The passenger door opens.

JACK

"Sparky."

After six months in hiding, I'd almost forgotten about my ex-cellmate, about the promise I'd broken and the cash I'd stolen, but clearly, Sparky's forgotten nothing. He looks more wired than the last time I saw him. His eyes are bloodshot, wide and wild. He's wearing a tattered long-sleeved top and canvas pants. He's holding a gun at my face, held sideways just like the gangster he is.

"Get out of the car."

I hold up my hands submissively and slide across the seat. "Take it easy. I'm doing what you tell me."

Megan is frozen in place. She doesn't slide out the car, and she doesn't get out the other side, even though it's now unlocked. We don't know what the other man in the car is going to do. She's paralyzed with fear. I don't blame her.

Don't move, Megan. It's me he wants.

I get out of the car and stand slowly. There's a gun in my face, but I'm only scared for Megan. I don't want her to pay for my mistakes.

"What's this about, man?"

"Are you fucking kidding me?" Sparky punctuates each work with a jerk of his gun. His finger is on the trigger. He could pull it at any moment. "You fucked me over when you let that bitch live. You stole from me—from *me*, the only one who gave half a fuck about your sorry ass, who gave you a place to live. And now you've put Raynor behind bars so I'm out of work." He sniffs loudly and deeply, blinking at a hundred miles an hour. He can't stay still. He's visibly shaking and crazy restless.

"I was looking out for number one. The way you always told me."

"You were looking after some whore you set your eyes on. I could have got you better pussy at the Twilight Bar."

My chest tightens in anger. Sparky always knows just what to say to bring out the dark side of me that I try so hard to repress.

"I saved the life of an innocent woman. You gonna shoot me for that?"

The gun goes off, and I instantly feel a blinding pain in my shoulder, enough to knock me back but not knock me down. I clamp my hand down over the wound, feeling the hot blood pumping out beneath my fingers. It's already soaking through my shirt.

"That's what betrayal feels like." Sparky takes a step closer to me, still pointing that gun at me. He's out of his mind in a murderous rage. He shoots at me again. This time a bullet just grazes my shoulder, close to my jugular.

"Calm down, man. Calm down."

How many more bullets can be in that gun? If I could get him to shoot me four more times, Megan will be safe.

My breathing is so shallow I might as well be holding my breath. I force myself to stay on my feet and stagger forward toward Sparky, even though my shoulder is in agony. I swear I can feel the bullet lodged beneath my collarbone like a penknife under my skin. Every breath is painful.

Sparky raises his hands—and the gun—in the air as he goes on a drug-fueled rant about his sorry life.

"I look out for everyone, but when is anyone ever looking out for Sparky, huh? Who'd you think they're going to come after now, hmm? Sparky. They're all going to be looking to point the finger at someone. I'm the one who let Megan get away. I'm the one who brought you in just for you to turn on me.

"You took my money, man. *You*. Took. *My*. Money. Ten years stuck together between the same four walls. Ten years of brotherhood and you fuck me over and steal from me."

"You're right. I'm a piece of shit, man. I let you down."

"And the second guy I send? He can't do the job either. I guess I just have to do it myself."

Sparky strides past me, arm outstretched, toward the car where Megan is still inside. I can't let him do that. I put all my strength into plowing into his body, pummeling him to the ground. He falls hard, and we start to fight.

I've got to get that gun.

Screams tear from my body as I fight him. Every movement sends white-hot agony through my body. The strength in my arm comes only from adrenaline; the muscles feel like they're shredded beneath my skin. It's willpower alone that's giving me the power to hold him off.

"Run, Megan! Get out of here!"

I manage to get a hit in on Sparky's jaw. He's beneath me on the ground. The hit is enough to make him loosen his grip on the gun. I kick it as far away from us as I can while still holding him down.

Relief floods through me. Megan is out of the firing line, and the gun is out of Sparky's hand. I just need to hold my own in a fistfight until Khosa and his men get here.

Sparky reaches for something in the pocket of his pants. I see the gleam of the blade and hold my breath, ready to feel the knife in my side. Instead, I hear a gunshot but feel nothing.

I've not been shot. Neither has Sparky.

We both look for the source of the sound.

At some point, Megan has picked up the gun. She's standing with both hands wrapped around the base, both fingers on the trigger. She's aiming at Sparky.

"Get away from him."

Sparky falls back. I rise to my feet, staggering over to Megan and taking the gun from her hands. I keep it pointed at Sparky.

"It's over, man. It's done." I can hear the sirens in the distance now. Just like WITSEC—always two minutes too late. "That's the police. You're going back to the joint, buddy."

He falls to his knees, scrambling in the dust of the derelict nowhere we've found ourselves. He clasps his hands together in a pathetic prayer and begs me to let him go.

"Come on, Strike. You can't do this to me. Let me walk away. You'll never hear from me again."

I swallow. I'm betraying the only friend I ever had, but the call to redemption is stronger than any loyalty I have to this lowlife.

"That's not going to happen. You're dangerous. I can't trust you not to hurt someone again."

"You two will never see my face again."

"There are more people in this world than Megan and me. You're a danger to everyone. You're the poison that runs through Baltimore. People like you are the reason all of us get stuck there. Someone's got to clean that place up. Consider this my contribution."

"You think you're better than me? *You're a murderer*." He

turns to Megan, hoping to drag me through the dirt as his last stand. "He killed his stepfather. He tried to kill you."

Megan calmly folds her arms across her chest. "I was in court. I heard everything. I know exactly what he's done."

Sparky laughs a psychotic, high-pitched cackle. "Stupid bitch. Need another murderer to get your rocks off now that Calvin's behind bars? Can only get off with a killer, huh? That's some kink you've got."

I cock the gun. I'm about ready to shoot Sparky. "Don't talk to her like that."

Megan places her hand on my shoulder, making me wince. The wound is just above my collarbone. "He's not worth it. The police are almost here. You've got another chance. With me."

I put the safety back on, but I don't move my aim until Khosa and his officers arrive. There's a whole fleet of federal vehicles—five in total. A crowd of officers moves toward Sparky.

He should have stayed down. Instead, Sparky pitches for one final act of self-destruction, as he was born to do, and lunges at the first cop to approach him with the same knife he tried to stop me with.

No less than four officers shoot at the same time to protect their fellow officer. Sparky collapses in a pool of his own blood, four bullet holes in his chest. Dead before he hits the ground.

MEGAN

I'VE BEEN WAITING for hours at JW Ruby Memorial Hospital. Khosa has been keeping an eye on me as I pace up and down the corridors, still covered in Jack's blood from when I grasped onto him as the officers surrounded us and ambulances flooded in. In fact, a whole fleet of officers is stationed on this one hospital corridor. Only authorized personnel are allowed in and out. Jack and I have both been targeted, and nowhere in the world is safe.

Although it's over now.

Or is it? I thought it was over when Calvin's verdict was read. Maybe it will never truly be over. Maybe I'll always be looking over my shoulder. It doesn't matter—as long as Jack is with me, I know I'll sleep soundly. He is my protector. He's not failed me yet.

"Jesus," I mutter to myself.

Khosa's head snaps up. He marches over to me to lay a hand on my shoulder. "Are you alright?"

"I'm fine." I'm restless. "When are they going to let me see him?"

"Maybe it's best you go to the safehouse and get some rest."

"I'm not going anywhere." I scuff my foot against the linoleum and look up at Khosa resentfully. "I know you don't like him."

Khosa scoffs and removes his hand from my shoulder. "I don't *want* to like him because my job is to keep you safe. But he just proved himself by saving you again."

"He wants to be one of the good guys."

Khosa offers a rare smile. "If there's anyone who can help him be a better man, it's you."

I blush. "Thank you. I think he deserves a fresh start every bit as much as me."

"If life with Jack is what it takes to give you a happy new life, then I support your decision to be with him. And I'll do what it takes to help keep you both safe."

"Thank you, Abdel. Life with Jack, or should I say Colin, is what I want."

* * *

Jack is pale, but he doesn't look as frail and broken as I expected after his surgery. He's wearing a hospital gown, those tattoos on display on his left arm. His right arm is in a sling, protecting the fresh surgery site.

He looks groggy, but he's awake. He tries to sit up when I enter, grunting with the effort.

"Lay back," I tell him. "It's okay."

He does as he's told and falls back onto the pillow to rest. He closes his eyes for a moment. When I see him, my heart lurches forward like it's trying to jump out my chest to reach him. The yearning is unspeakable. The relief is overwhelming.

He's alive and safe and will soon be on the road to recovery. I pull up a chair at the side of his hospital bed and clasp his hand in mine.

"The doctor said the surgery went excellently. They retrieved the bullet and five bone fragments from your collarbone."

"The surgeon told me that bullet shredded quite a bit of muscle when it ricocheted around in there."

"But no organ damage, thank God."

"Silver lining, hey?"

My chin begins to wobble. I've been holding in my worry and shock ever since I heard the first gunshot fired. I pull myself up onto the mattress beside Jack and being careful not to disturb his injury, I gently lay my body over his, cuddling up against him.

He rests his face against my hair and breathes in the scent of me.

"When that car stopped, I had no idea how this was going to end."

"I should have known you'd save us both."

"Me? You're the one who got the gun."

"Only after you'd been shot."

Jack places a finger under my chin to tilt my face upward to look at him. "You saved my life today."

"You saved me first."

He closes his good arm around me, wincing at the pain of the movement. I try to bear my own weight to make sure I'm not putting any pressure on him, but all I want to do is curl up against him and feel safe and small in his arms.

"It'll be a story to tell the grandkids, that's for sure."

I laugh. "You still want to stick around me when I cause this much trouble?"

"Life was boring as hell on the inside. I could do with a little excitement."

"I've had enough excitement to last me a lifetime." I turn

my face and gently stroke a finger over Jack's dry, pale lips before leaning forward to kiss them. "I'm happy to by Lucy Goody, or Amy Blythe, or whoever I have to be to be able to bring the world to a halt for five minutes."

"Colin Meyers has survived to live another day, too." Jack's gaze grows glassy. "Unlike Sparky."

"He dug his own grave," I say softly. "He pulled a knife in front of two dozen police."

"I know."

Jack looks bereft, and I'm not sure I understand why. Whoever it was that pulled a gun on us was a madman on Calvin's payroll. I feel safer knowing he's not breathing anymore, but Jack looks distraught.

"Sparky was that middleman I told you about. My cell-mate for ten years."

"A friend?"

"He wasn't a friend. He wasn't family. He was Sparky. He was a sadist and an asshole, but he was the only person in my life for a long, long time. He died hunting me down. I feel like I might as well have pulled the trigger myself."

I stroke Jack's hair softly. "You can't blame yourself."

"He had his own demons, like everyone else."

"He had his own choices, too. You're living proof that you can choose to walk away."

Jack takes a long deep breath then lets it out slowly. "I guess."

"You're not on your own, you know." I run the back of my hand softly across his cheek, both reveling in touching him and trying to offer some comfort. "I'm here. Whatever comes for us now, we're going to face together."

He clenches his jaw. I almost think I can see tears welling in his eyes. "Is anything that easy?" He lets his head fall back heavily on the pillow. "Am I kidding myself that I can have a normal life; that we're going to make it? Everything in my life goes up in flames the second any small spark of joy ignites. I don't even know where to begin living a normal life."

His soul speaks to mine. I'm not as good at holding back the tears as Jack is. Mine roll down my cheeks.

"Don't say that, Jack. Because if it's true for you, it's true for me too—and I've *got* to believe that things get better. I'm sorry you lost your friend, but you don't need to fear the future. I've had every horrible thing come my way—kicks and punches, loneliness and despair, wanting to end it all—and I've felt hopeless...but I don't with you." I kiss his cheek, then his forehead; his lips. I plant kisses all over his face. "You give me hope."

JACK

ONE MONTH later

Megan's home—my new home—is not too far from Fron-
tenac State Park, and the peace of the reserve seems to carry
over to all the streets around it. There is calm in the air;
quiet. I can't hear sirens wailing in the distance or mysterious
bangs that could be gunshots. I can't smell urine or cannabis.
I can't see graffiti. Everything is clean and fresh and perfect.

I stand staring at the front door of this new chapter of my
life. The house is small and sweet with pastel blue wood
paneling and a white side-porch with three little steps up to
the door. There are trees on either side of the building,
framing the fairytale home in between. There is lace at the
windows; a pot full of flowers.

There is no shouting inside. I can't hear people swearing.
I can't smell booze or smoke.

Inside, I feel fifteen again—a child who was always afraid
to go home. I stare at that house with the same sense of
wonder as a child. For the first time in my life, I'm standing
in front of my own sanctuary; a real home. And inside, the
woman of my dreams is waiting.

Megan and I haven't seen each other in a month. After she visited me in the hospital, she was whisked away once more, and it is only now—when my wounds have healed and the storm has passed—that I can see her once more.

I take the three steps up to the door and knock.

The door is instantly thrown open. Megan throws herself into my arms, threading her arms around my neck, kissing me deeply and kicking up one leg behind her like in the movies. She almost bowls me over.

I drop the bag I'd been holding and wrap her up in both arms. I squeeze with all my strength, and it's still not tight enough. I never want to let go.

"You're really here," she whispers. She smiles up at me, and her eyes are shining with happy tears. "I've missed you. Come inside."

She takes me by the hand and leads me inside. "I've prepared everything for you so it feels like home." She gestures to the shoe rack by the door. "I've left space for your shoes." She drags me through to the kitchen. "There are cold beers in the fridge." Through to the living room; she points at a shelving unit. "The complete Lord of the Rings trilogy on DVD. And there's one more thing."

Megan takes my shoulders and spins me to look at the wall behind the duck-egg blue sofa with flowery cushions. Above it is a huge, framed piece of art—dozens, maybe a hundred, vintage playing cards on display in a giant frame.

I turn back to look at her.

She's waiting for my reaction. Her face is flushed with anticipation. She bites down on her lip, twirling a strand of long—much longer—blonde hair around her finger. Nothing in this house is as beautiful as her. She's wearing a pink chiffon dress that floats with each movement.

"It's perfect."

"You really like it?"

"It's home."

She steps forward, places her hands on either side of my face and kisses me softly. "It's our home."

I wrap my arm around her waist and pull her close. I've hungered for her kiss for four long weeks; twenty-nine days, to be exact. I've woken up during the long hospital nights dreaming of her touch. I've caught her scent on the wind like a ghost more time than I can count. My imagination has kept her with me all this time, but now she's really here.

"I love you." I say it, then kiss her deeply. Her mouth is sweet, and my kiss steals her breath away. It escapes her lungs in a blissful sigh, warm against my face. I bury my fingers in her hair and kiss her cheek, her neck, her collarbone.

She buries her face in my shoulder and breathes heavily as my mouth traces her body. She runs her fingers through my hair.

"I've missed you," she whispers.

"Not as much as I've missed you. It's not possible."

MEGAN

HE PLACES his hands on my waist and lifts me up like I weigh nothing. He doesn't even wince with his injured shoulder. It's like he can see and feel nothing but me.

I can't see anything else either. The second Jack appeared at the door, everything else fell away. I opened the door and saw my future, my past, and every dream I've ever had standing there in the flesh.

Flesh. I want his body on mine. I want to touch him. I want to feel his skin bare against mine.

I wrap my legs around his waist, and he carries me through the house to the bedroom I've just shown him upstairs. The bedsheets are immaculate, prepared—brown, caramel and gold.

He lays me down like I'm fragile and precious. There is a new softness in him. Every touch feels like he's cherishing me.

"I've pictured you every day and every night," he tells me, "but you're even more beautiful than I remembered."

His words are honey to my ears. I practically moan just at

the sound of him speaking. I've longed for his love and his comfort for so long.

Jack runs a palm along my calf and upward to my inner thigh. He lets out a long, low breath of desire, then lowers his head to kiss where his hands have touched. He kisses up my legs and then between them. He hooks a finger into my panties and pulls them down, kissing the bare skin beneath them before leaning across the bed where I lay to kiss me on the lips.

Now his body is so close to mine I can feel the heat of him. The space between our bodies is burning. There is heat in the air. I raise my head to kiss him on the lips. I go from closing my eyes in bliss to staring into his eyes in wonder; in disbelief that he's finally here and we're really together at last.

Jack's kiss is tender at first. His warm tongue is seeking and hungry. I part my lips to let him kiss me deeply. I cling onto his shoulders, then reach for the hem of his gray T-shirt to pull it over his head.

His body is only a little less toned from his time in a hospital bed. The muscles still remain, even that shadow of a six-pack. The only real change is the pinkish scar above his collarbone, still red and healing.

I press my palms against his chest. I can feel his heart beating under my hands. Its rhythm soothes and calms me. I relax back onto the fresh sheets as Jack pulls my dress up over my head.

This time I'm ready to be seen. I'm wearing a white lace bra, although the matching panties are already on the floor. I see the arousal in Jack's eyes when his gaze drags over my body, drinking in every last inch of my skin.

"You're so fucking beautiful."

I smile and kiss him again. I could kiss him a thousand times and still crave the taste of him.

I reach for his belt buckle and slowly undo his pants. He

takes off his jeans, briefs, shoes, and socks. He's naked on top of me. I love the feeling of the weight of his body on mine like a comforting blanket, warm and heavy.

I wrap my arms around his body; his shoulders are so broad my hands can't meet, so I grasp at his back, digging my fingers into the hot, soft skin of his body.

Jack undoes my bra and slips it away from my body. He lowers his mouth to my breast and gently sucks at a nipple. The feeling sends pangs of arousal shooting through me. I grow wet as my nipples harden. I grasp at his hair; well-ready for another cut, but the perfect length to hold onto.

He presses a finger into me, sliding in easily with how wet I am already. He brushes his finger against my clit. I moan.

"I've missed that sound," he says in a low, husky voice full of desire. He kisses me. "I can't wait to hear it every day."

He firmly strokes my clit until I start to squirm, then he rubs faster.

"Don't stop." The feeling builds and I start to gasp, clinging onto his shoulder. "Don't stop! Don't stop!"

He grins wickedly and continues until he brings me to orgasm. The feeling sends tremors through my body, leaving my legs weak.

I pull myself back on the bed and open my legs. "I want you so badly."

"I'm all yours."

Jack positions himself over me then slides inside in one smooth, deep thrust.

Ecstasy.

I pin my thighs against his hips, wanting to guide his body into me, wanting to hold him close. I raise my upper body to make sure I don't stop kissing him. I want to taste him, feel him, and have him inside me all at the same time. The scent of his cologne is delicious.

I let out whimpers of delight as Jack takes me, bringing to life weeks and months of fantasy and memory.

Before he comes, he rolls onto his back and holds out his arms to me. I don't waste any time in straddling him and sliding down onto his thick cock. It's an amazing view when I'm riding him. I can see every one of his rippling muscles, his strong arms. I can watch his expression as he closes his eyes in bliss and groans.

I rock my hips against him. I can feel him so deep inside me. I bow down over him, letting my hair sweep across his chest. I kiss him, pushing down further, pushing him deeper inside me.

He grasps at my hips, urging me to rock faster. I take his lead and sway my hips to the rhythm his touch demands.

"That feels amazing."

I bask in his pleasure and throw my head back in pleasure of my own. I move as he urges me, rocking harder and faster, taking him deeper until a moan rises up from deep within him and his body shudders underneath me, his fingers digging into my skin.

He comes with a cry, and I bite down on my smile. That sound is sexy as hell.

I move off his body and lie beside him. I could cry from how happy I feel right now. We're both clammy and naked and sitting on crumpled bedsheets. I nestle up against him, laying my head down on his chest and hearing his heart beat.

"I love you, too, Jack."

EPILOGUE

Megan

Two years later.

Jack walks in with his carpentry toolkit in one hand and a bag of groceries in the other. He finds me in the kitchen and first kisses my lips and then my stomach.

"How are my two favorite girls today? Something smells amazing."

I laugh and gaze at him with the same adoring gaze as every day. In the two years since we started our lives in Minnesota, Jack—or should I say Colin—has proven a million times over that he's every bit the good and decent man I believed him to be.

He works hard, he spoils me, and he still makes love to me like it's our first time every time. I'm surprised I didn't get pregnant sooner.

"We don't know it's a girl yet." I place my hand protectively over my bump. I can't quite feel the baby kicking yet, but soon my little bean will be frolicking about in there.

"I know, I know," Jack smiles. "I've just got this feeling."

He places his paper bag of groceries down on the table

and starts pulling out items. "Spinach, for iron. Salmon for Omega 3. Pre-natal vitamins from the pharmacy. Smoked Cheddar, and..." He pulls the last item out with a flourish. "The new *IT* movie."

I giggle. "Do you think all these horror movies are good for the baby?"

Jack pats my belly lovingly. "She's going to be a tough girl, like her mom." He kisses my forehead affectionately. "Don't worry. There'll be plenty of time for *My Little Pony* when she's out. How long will dinner be?"

"About an hour."

"Perfect. I'll be in the nursery."

"Jack!"

"What?"

"You spend every waking hour decorating that room."

"I want it to be perfect for her."

"Or him. You'll wear yourself out."

He pauses and offers that same cheeky, adorable smile he always does when he's being too damned sweet and loyal and it's making me worry about him. "I enjoy it."

"I know you do." I sigh, resigned, and place my ladle down on the counter. "Don't work too hard. You'll do your shoulder in."

He rolls his shoulder back pointedly and then shows off his guns. "I'm strong as an ox."

Jack goes upstairs to continue painting—or maybe he's doing more carving on that handmade crib that's been his labor of love for the past six weeks.

I hum to myself as I cook. Today, like every day, I'm calm and happy and free. As I lift a spoon to stir, I find myself staring at the engagement ring on my finger once more. Every time it catches the light, I watch it sparkle. It's not the diamond that makes my heart melt but what that ring means.

Not so long ago, my life was dark. Every moment was

lived in the shadows, spent in fear. Even when Jack came into my life, there was so much uncertainty. Our path was littered with conspiracy and deceit. Our lives were interwoven and torn apart again and again to create a patchy fabric of a romance.

When he finally came to Minnesota, I shared the same fears he did, no matter how I might have comforted him. I, too, was scared that this happy life would never work for us. Like Jack, I wondered if we were too broken and too filled with darkness to live in the light.

Yet, here we are. The last couple of years have rolled by without drama or violence. And it's been *so easy*. Every day with Jack is a joy. I feel safe, loved, and like I belong. He makes me feel whole and makes this house feel like a home.

About eighteen months ago, I found a job working retail at a local bath bomb store. Within six months, I was promoted to assistant manager.

I love it.

It has a lot of the same perks as hairdressing; I get to meet lots of different people and chat away all day. Plus, I love the products and get to bring home a ton of free bath bombs, essential oils, and body creams. One day I'll smell like a peach and the next day like "Cosmic Horizon." Best of all, when I leave the store, work stays at work.

I usually get home about an hour before Jack, which is when I'll start cooking and doing some housework. By the time he comes home, we have nothing on our minds and can be free to chat over dinner, watch horror movies, share stories about our days, and enjoy each other's company.

Not one day has been stale. The routine has never gotten old.

I still feel the same butterflies when Jack walks into a room as I always did. Even more so now, as I'm not just seeing my lover, but my fiancé and the father of my child.

Jack's going from strength to strength in his work. He started out carving pieces in the garage and selling them online, but now he has his own store and has gathered a lot of interest. He'd probably have gotten a lot further if he could publicize a bit more. As it is, he keeps his head down and face out of the paper. He lets his work speak for itself so nobody with bad intentions can ever find us.

There's been no sign of any of Calvin's cronies since Sparky was shot. For the first six months, I was still looking over my shoulder, but now everything that happened before feels like a bad dream.

Calvin is behind bars where he should be, and Jack and I are living good lives.

Sometimes we talk about how much life has changed. I've turned from the rebel girl in leather pants to the submissive gangster's lover to a mother-to-be and fantastic baker. Jack's gone from aspiring artist, to teen felon, to would-be assassin, to family man.

It hasn't been a conventional road to happy, but my God are we happy.

We're planning a winter wedding at the lighthouse at Lake Pepin. It will be a few months after the baby is born. I'm not buying a wedding dress until the week before—just in case I get huge during this pregnancy.

The only thing that makes me sad is how isolated this child will be. He or she will have no grandparents and no aunties or uncles. I'm afraid that mine and Jack's errant ways will leave our child with no family. I feel guilty for that, but there's nothing I can do. In Witness Protection, I don't have the option of reaching out to my parents now—and maybe it's for the best. They wouldn't recognize me now anyway. I've come so far.

Jack doesn't share my guilt. He always reminds me how happy we are.

"There is more love between you and me than in a house with eight grandparents, three dozens aunts and uncles, and a third cousin twice removed."

I like the way he sees things—he's not wrong. The love in this home is enough to last a thousand lifetimes, and I get to fit it all into one.

We live in a beautiful home, we both have jobs we love, we have a child on the way, and a wedding planned. Everything is perfect.

Jack and Megan, Lucy and Colin. Who the hell cares?

As long as we're together.

NEWSLETTER

Sign up for my newsletter to get information on new releases.

If you liked this story, please leave a review of this book on Amazon, and recommend it to your friends!

Want Free Books?

I'm looking for people who want a sneak preview of my books before they are released, and can write reviews of the books on Amazon.

Visit http://lisalace.com/arc/ to learn more!

ALSO BY LISA LACE

Auxem

Ayrie

Anders

Alien Prince's Mate

Avren

TerraMates

Water World Warrior

Taken

Water World Confidential

Alpha's Enslaved Bride

Auctioned to the Alpha

Wrong Alien

Naima

Craving

Irresistible

Warrior Invasion

Origins

Savage Alien

Auxem

Claimed by the Alien Warlord

Burning Metal

Cyborg Heat

Cyborg Fury

Cyborg Seduction

The Surtu

Warriors of Surtu

Kidnapped by Surtu

Captured by the Alien King

Captured by the Alien King

Mated to the Alien King

Desert World Savages

Desert World Savages

Queen of the Savages

Copyright © 2019 by Lisa Lace

All rights reserved.

This book is a work of fiction. The characters, events and dialog found within the story are of the author's imagination and are not to be construed as real. Any resemblance to actual events or persons, either living or deceased, is completely coincidental.

No part of this book may be reproduced in any form or by any electronic or mechanical means, including information storage and retrieval systems, without written permission from the author, except for the use of brief quotations in a book review.

62345882R00116

Made in the USA
Middletown, DE
23 August 2019